Nine
SONS

COLLECTED MYSTERIES

WENDY HORNSBY
(Photography by David Bauer)

Nine SONS

COLLECTED MYSTERIES

WENDY HORNSBY

Crippen & Landru Publishers
Norfolk, Virginia
2002

Cover painting by Barbara Mitchell

Cover design by Deborah Miller

Crippen & Landru logo by Eric D. Greene

ISBN (limited edition): 1-885941-65-X
ISBN (trade edition): 1-885941-66-8

FIRST EDITION
10 9 8 7 6 5 4 3 2 1

Crippen & Landru Publishers, Inc.
P. O. Box 9315
Norfolk, VA 23505
USA
www.crippenlandru.com
CrippenL@Pilot.Infi.Net

In memory of Fern Nelson, story teller

CONTENTS

INTRODUCTION

Maybe a hundred times, at workshops and interviews and luncheon speeches, I have said that the difference between writing a short story and writing a book is something like the difference between writing haiku and composing epic verse. There is some truth there. In a book, the author has plenty of time to ramble around plot and character and setting. Short stories require precision; every phrase has to be to the point. But the differences are far more than length, or scope.

Before I begin writing a book, I usually go through a long sort of rumination about the way people behave in some circumstance. Then I do research, a discussion of which follows. And then I think some more: who will populate the world created in the book, how will they make my point for me, how will they be changed?

Short stories come to me like snapshots; bright, vivid pictures that I see whole from the very first. The story behind the snapshot is insistent and intense. It needs to be written quickly, even if that means interrupting a work in progress. That is, I have to stop working on a book I've been toiling on for months and write the story, quick. Forget the haiku analogy. The difference between writing a short story and a book is more like the difference between a one-night stand and a long-term, committed relationship.

Where do these flashes come from? Out of the ether is the best answer I can give you. Or, as happened to Dante, "*In media res.*" In the middle of things, when least expected. As unexpected gifts, stories just seem to land upon me. They always have.

WENDY HORNSBY

A good part of my coming up was spent in the backseat of the family car — always a shiny Chrysler that was about two lanes wide, my sister beside me, our little brother in front with our parents — while we traveled around the country looking for adventure, camping out, gathering material for stories that we would tell over and over later.

It seems to me that in the retelling everything that happened to us became just a little funnier, hotter, more beautiful or more dangerous, or just simply more interesting than the original experiences probably ever could have been. Like the retouched portraits hanging on the family room wall, our stories had an altered, prettied up truth.

Both of my parents were — my father still is — masters of the art of the embellished story, though their styles could not be more different.

My father's childhood I know as a series of rich scenes that string across the map from northern Kansas to a boxcar in Nevada — where his brother, his guardian then, built bridges for Union Pacific — to Montebello, California where he survived the BIG ONE, the '33 earthquake, to the San Joaquin Valley, and eventually to the South Pacific during the last great war. Dad has some classic stories we ask for over and over, like the one about Granddaddy Ole, a professional wrestler in his youth, and his match with the Indian who ate too many beans for dinner.

My father's tales are usually pretty funny, told with an amazing variety of voices and accents and sound effects. They're earthy; a lot of them have to do with eating beans. I love every one of them.

As good as my father's stories are, though, it was always my mother's stories that stuck in the mind. Not because her stories were inherently better, but only because she didn't play fair. Even when they were funny, her stories had a dark side to them, a back story she would not reveal beyond vague hints. The rest I'll tell you later, she would say. When you're older. When I'm ready. When all the players are gone.

I kept asking her to pay up. I nagged. What happened to Irma the night the cutter came for her? What did you overhear Dr. Gimby tell Uncle Bill? The baby the Peruvian woman tried to thrust on Grandfather at the boat, whose was it?

Now and then, nagging bore fruit. I begged, pitifully, for maybe twenty years before she gave me all of the story that became "Nine Sons." After she gave it to me, I had to think about this gift for a while before I was ready to write it down. I was in the middle of writing my second book when the story emerged, whole, insisting to be told. I gave in, took a break from the book, and wrote it. Then I let the first version age before I rewrote it in the final form you will find among the stories collected here.

To tell you the truth, the story behind "Nine Sons" and its many versions have resided with me for so long now that I cannot with any confidence separate the pure thread of the original from the fiction you will read. Be assured that embedded somewhere in the embroidery Mother did in the telling, and I did in the retelling, there is a parallel that did in fact occur. A boy like Janos, his sister, his mother, the funeral — over which my grandfather presided — all are real, in their way. So is the linoleum floor. Of course, there is more to the story than you'll find here. But we'll talk about that later. When you're older. When I'm ready ...

"High Heels in the Headliner" had very different origins. It came out of the process of researching Los Angeles and its seamier denizens for the Maggie MacGowen books.

After I won the Edgar for "Nine Sons," an interviewer sent from National Public Radio described me as soft-spoken, genteel college professor Wendy Hornsby. That description bothered me a great deal because I had come to see myself as part of the noir tradition of my native city, Los Angeles. I wanted to be as a tough a cookie as is my series protagonist, Maggie MacGowen. Had I failed?

This is the sad truth: my whole life has been awfully goddamn genteel. Like Thea in "High Heels Through the Headliner," when I wanted to write about crime I had to go out and find the real world. I talked to people: "You've seen the other side. What's it like over there?" I am endlessly amazed by what people will tell me when I say I'm working on a book.

Cops, D.A.'s, criminals, slick blonde moms sitting in Eddie Bauer chairs along girl's soccer game sidelines, among others, spill it to me. "Worked Metro, SWAT, during the SLA shoot-out ..." "It wasn't my fault ..." "My life is wilder than a Danielle Steele plot ..."

"I'm working on a book" got me an introduction to the judge in a capital murder case I had been following for two years, from the day the body was found. When the D.A. set up the meeting with the judge for me, all that I really wanted to know was, where do judges lunch? They seem so lonely when the D.A.'s and defense attorneys and the detectives stand around court swapping jokes or making plans for lunch — take the Red Line out to MacArthur Park together for pastrami at Langer's, or walk down to the Civic Center mall for fast food. The judge can't go with them. Do they feel left out? (The answers are, judges go together to elegant places like Saratoga, or they get their clerks to bring them up something from the cafeteria. And sometimes it is lonely if there isn't another judge available; to paraphrase Ben Franklin, they hang together, or they hang separately.)

I asked a simple question. What I got was an absolutely fascinating discourse on one man's progress from federal prosecutor to law prof to cute-as-a-bug judge (swear to God, he looks enough like my classical history prof — upon whom I once had a pathetic crush — to be family). He told me about the mobster over whose trial he presided, who said to him, with a smile, "I know where you live." And about the counterfeiting case he prosecuted, and lost, to the defense attorney in the murder case before him.

During an interview that lasted less than an hour, I learned enough about judges to fuel a chapter or two: portrait of beautiful wife on the credenza, the view across Chinatown from his chambers, the back hallway that leads to the chambers of another judge (the Rodney King case judge), the relationship with his clerk. He handed over a lot of grist for a fiction miller.

And so it goes. I have learned that I can call upon just about anyone, explain what I want, and get cooperation. I call the coroner's retired chief of forensic science services and leave a message on his machine: "I have a body that's been in sea water for eight weeks. What does he look like?" The answer is in my book, *Midnight Baby*.

I get a late-night call from a twenty-year LAPD cop who has been promoted and reassigned to Newton Station (Rootin' Shootin' Newton). The dog he worked with for six years has retired to his back yard and the cop is working with humans again. He isn't sure how he feels about it. So, he waxes nostalgic about his old partners and pranks pulled on patrol duty, and about cops who died with their boots on. The things I learned ...

I soak up details big and small. The assistant D.A. takes me up to the sad little balcony on the eighteenth floor of the Criminal Courts Building where he smokes his cigarettes. Remember sneaking a joint? Same atmosphere.

The victim of a jailhouse rape tells me more than I really want to know. The keeper of property in the morgue shows me the box that holds the skull of an actor who was fooling around with a movie prop revolver loaded with blanks. It's all good stuff, and I feel grateful for the help.

Now and then I hear, "Don't tell anyone." I always say, "Sure I won't tell anyone except thousands of readers. If you don't want it repeated, don't tell me."

I think people need to talk about what they do. And when their stories end up in print, however altered, there is a special satisfaction.

The exchange works both ways. Sometimes I have a feeling people plant stories with me, or their version of stories, just to get them aired.

Honest to God, an investigator for the D.A., an LAPD vet, six-five, two-eighty — paints sounding whales for a hobby — told me something no one ought to know: "During the SLA shoot-out, Nancy Ling Perry came out of that burning house to surrender. Threw down her carbine, raised her hands, she was giving herself up. I know for a fact that the cop standing in the backyard said, 'Die, bitch,' and shot her six times, severed her fucking spine. His partner kicked her discarded carbine under her to cover himself, but no one questioned that it wasn't a justified hit."

I said, "Is this something I can repeat?"

He said, "No way". But he knew I was working on a book, *77th Street Requiem*, in which I had made Nancy Ling Perry a suspect in a cop killing; a fictional version of a real-life event. And I real-life believe she had something to do with the murder. She's dead, I can't ask her for confirmation. And that's too bad. I used the secret revelation about how she died, and the man who gave it to me likes the way I told his story.

Now and then, I have a pang about appropriating a story that didn't begin as mine, or Maggie MacGowen's, or, in the case of "High Heels Through the Headliner," as Thea's. That pang is where the germ for "High Heels" came from. I hope I could never use anyone as wantonly as Thea does, but I am as eager to find the real scoop as she is. This also is the truth: I honestly don't know how far I'd go.

INTRODUCTION

The essay, "Wendy goes to the Morgue," will take you through one of my research adventures.

Every story here, and it isn't a lengthy oeuvre, began as a snapshot. "New Moon and Rattlesnakes" occurred to me when I watched a desert truckstop prostitute solicit. I thought about both how dangerous her job was and how anonymous she could become. "Ghost Caper" came from an idea for a book that never happened, based on a real spoiled cop, now serving life without possibility of parole, who engaged in petty burglaries that seemed unnecessarily risky and small-time when compared to his other crimes. What would motivate him to break into the homes of sleeping people, I wondered? "Naked Giant": drive down California's Big Sur and try to avoid thoughts of danger or voluptuous giants. I say it can't be done. "The Last is Adoration" came from watching a murder trial. I have tried to present the story to you as it would unfold as testimony from various sources. In a murder trial, one voice is always missing.

Two stories here are different from the others. My daughter Alyson and I have been asked, twice, to co-author stories. The process of collaboration was interesting. Both stories are about mother and daughter pairs. In both, divorce is the specter. None of the women we wrote about is us. None of these things happened. Exactly.

That's the thing about fiction, isn't it? None of it happened. Exactly.

Wendy Hornsby
Long Beach, California
September 2001

NINE SONS

I saw Janos Bonachek's name in the paper this morning. There was a nice article about his twenty-five years on the federal bench, his plans for retirement. The Boy Wonder, they called him, but the accompanying photograph showed him to be nearly bald, a wispy white fringe over his ears the only remains of his once remarkable head of yellow hair.

For just a moment, I was tempted to write him, or call him, to put to rest forever questions I had about the death that was both a link and a wedge between us. In the end I didn't. What was the point after all these years? Perhaps Janos's long and fine career in the law was sufficient atonement, for us all, for events that happened so long ago.

The incident occurred on an otherwise ordinary day. It was April, but Spring was still only a tease. If anything stood out among the endless acres of black mud and gray slush, it was two dabs of bright color: first the blue crocus pushing through a patch of dirty snow then the bright yellow head of Janos Bonachek as he ran along the line of horizon toward his parent's farm after school. Small marvels, maybe, the spring crocus and young Janos, but in that frozen place, and during those hard times, surely they were miracles.

The year was 1934, the depths of the Great Depression. Times were bad, but in the small farm town where I had been posted by the school board, hardship was an old acquaintance.

I had arrived the previous September, fresh from teacher college, with a new red scarf in my bag and the last piece of my birthday cake. At twenty, I wasn't much older than my high-school-age pupils.

Janos was ten when the term began, and stood exactly the height of ripe wheat. His hair was so nearly the same gold as the bearded grain that he could run through the uncut fields and be no more noticeable than the ripples made by a prairie breeze. The wheat had to be mown before Janos could be seen at all.

On the northern Plains, the season for growing is short, a quick breath of summer between the Spring thaw and the first frost of Fall. Below the surface of the soil, and within the people who forced a living from it, there seemed to be a layer that never had time to warm all the way through. I believe to this day that if the winter hadn't been so long, the chilling of the soul so complete, we would not have been forced to bury Janos Bonachek's baby sister.

Janos came from a large family, nine sons. Only one of them, Janos, was released from chores to attend school regularly. Even then, he brought work with him in the form of his younger brother, Boya. Little Boya was that year four or five. He wasn't as brilliant as Janos, but he tried hard. Tutored and cajoled by Janos, Boya managed to skip to the second grade reader that year.

Around Halloween, that first year, Janos was passed up to me by the elementary grades teacher. She said she had nothing more to teach him. I don't know that I was any better prepared to teach him than she was, except that the high school textbooks were on the shelves in my room. I did my best.

Janos was a challenge. He absorbed everything I had to offer and demanded more, pushing me in his quiet yet insistent way to explain or to find out. He was eager for everything. Except geography. There he was a doubter. Having lived his entire life on a flat expanse of prairie, Janos would not believe that the earth was a sphere, or that there were bodies of water vaster than the wheat fields that stretched past his horizon. The existence of mountains, deserts, and oceans he had to take on faith, as I did the heavenly world the nuns taught me about in catechism.

Janos was an oddball to his classmates, certainly. I can still see that shiny head bent close to his books, the brow of his pinched little face furrowed as he took in a new set of universal truths from the world beyond the Central Grain Exchange. The other students deferred to him, respected him, though they never played with him. He spent recesses and lunch periods sitting on the school's front stoop, waiting for me to ring the big brass bell and let him back inside. I wonder how that affected him as a judge, this boy who never learned how to play.

Janos shivered when he was cold, but he seemed otherwise oblivious to external discomfort or appearances. Both he and Boya came to school barefoot until there was snow on the ground. Then they showed up in mismatched boots sizes too big. Yet, no one called attention to their shabbiness, which I found singular. Janos's coat, even in blizzards, was an old gray blanket that I'm sure he slept under at night. His straight yellow hair stuck out in chunks as if it had been scythed like the wheat. He never acknowledged that he was in any way different from his well-scrubbed classmates.

While this oblivion to discomfort gave Janos an air of stoic dignity, it did impose some hardship in me. When the blizzards came and I knew school should be closed, I went out anyway because I knew that Janos would be there, with Boya. If I didn't come to unlock the classroom, I was certain they would freeze waiting.

Getting to school in a blizzard was itself a challenge. I boarded in town with the doctor and his wife, my dear friend Martha. When the snow blew in blinding swirls and the road was impassable to any automobile, I would persuade the doctor to harness his team of plow horses to his cutter and drive me out. After the first trip, the doctor made only token protest: the boys had been at the school for some time before we arrived, huddled on the stoop like drifted snow.

Those snow days were the best days, alone, the boys and me. I would bring books from Martha's shelves, books not always on the school board approved list. We would read together, and talk about the world on the far side of the prairie and how one day we would see it for ourselves. We would, as the snow drifts piled up to the sills outside, try to imagine the sultry heat of the tropics, the pitch and roll of the oceans, men in pale suits in electricity-lit parlors discussing being and nothingness while they sipped hundred-year-old sherry.

We had many days together. That year the first snow came on All Saints Day and continued regularly until Good Friday. I would have despaired during the ceaseless cold if it weren't for Janos and the lessons I received at home on the evenings of those blizzardy days.

Invariably, on winter nights when the road was impassable and sensible people were at home before the fire, someone would call for the doctor's services. He would harness the cutter, and go. Martha, of course, couldn't sleep until she heard the cutter return. We would keep each other entertained, sometimes until after the sun came up.

Martha had gone to Smith or Vassar. I'm not sure which because Eastern girl's schools were so far from my experience that the names meant nothing to me then. She was my guide to the world I had only seen in magazines and slick-paged catalogues, where people were polished to a smooth and shiny perfection, where long underwear, if indeed any was worn, never showed below their hems. These people were oddly whole, no scars, no body parts lost to farm machinery. In their faces I saw a peace of mind I was sure left them open to the world of ideas. I longed for them, and was sure Martha did as well.

Martha took life in our small community with grace, though I knew she missed the company of other educated women. I had to suffice.

Just as I spent my days preparing Janos, Martha spent her evenings teaching me the social graces I would need if I were ever to make my escape. Perhaps I was not as quick a pupil as Janos, but I was as eager.

Lessons began in the attic where Martha kept her trunks. Packed in white tissue was the elegant trousseau she had brought with her from the East, gowns of wine-colored taffeta moiré and green velvet and a pink silk so fine I feared touching it with my callused hands.

I had never actually seen a live woman in an evening gown, though I knew Martha's gowns surpassed the mail order gowns that woman might order for an Eastern Star ritual, if she had money for ready-made.

Martha and I would put on the gowns and drink coffee with brandy and read to each other from Proust, or take turns at the piano. I might struggle through a Strauss waltz or the Fat Lady Polka. She played flawless Dvorak and Debussey. This was my finishing school, long nights in Martha's front parlor, waiting for the cutter to bring the doctor home, praying the cutter hadn't overturned, hoping the neighbor he had gone to tend was all right.

When he did return, his hands so cold he needed help out of his layers of clothes, Martha's standard greeting was, "Delivering Mrs. Bonachek?" This was a big joke to us, because, of course, Mrs. Bonachek delivered herself. No one knew how many pregnancies she had had beyond her nine living sons. Poor people, they were rich in sons.

That's what I kept coming back to that early spring afternoon as I walked away from the Bonachek farm. I had seen Janos running across the fields after school. If he hadn't been hurrying home to help his mother, then where had he gone? And where were his brothers?

It lay on my mind.

As I said, the day in question had been perfectly ordinary. I had stayed after my students to sweep the classroom, so it was nearly four before I started for home. As always, I walked the single-lane road toward town, passing the Bonachek farm about half way. Though underfoot, the black earth was frozen hard as tarmac, I was looking for signs of spring, counting the weeks until the end of the school term.

My feel were cold inside my new Sears and Roebuck boots and I was mentally drafting a blistering letter to the company. The catalogue copy had promised me boots that would withstand the coldest weather, so, as an act of faith in Sears, I had invested a good chunk of my slim savings for the luxury of warm feet. Perhaps the copywriter in a Chicago office could not imagine ground as cold as this road.

I watched for Janos's mother as I approached her farm. For three days running, I had seen Mrs. Bonachek working in the fields as I walked to school in the morning, and as I walked back to town in the dusky afternoon. There was no way to avoid her. The distance between the school and the Bonachek farm was uninterrupted by hill or wall or stand of trees.

Mrs. Bonachek would rarely glance up as I passed. Unlike the other parents, she never greeted me, never asked me how her boys were doing in school, never suggested I let them out earlier for farm chores. She knew little English, but neither did many of the other parents, or my own.

She was an enigma. Formless, colorless, Mrs. Bonachek seemed no more than a piece of the landscape as she spread seed grain onto the plowed ground from a big pouch in her apron. Wearing felt boots, she walked slowly along the straight furrows, her thin arm moving in a sweep as regular as any motor-powered machine.

Hers was an odd display of initiative, I thought. No one else was out in the fields yet. It seemed to me she risked losing her seed to mildew or to a last spring freeze by planting so early. Something else bothered me more. While I was a dairyman's daughter and knew little about growing wheat, I knew what was expected of farm children.

There were six in my family, my five brothers and myself. My mother never went to the barns alone when there was a child at hand. Mrs. Bonachek had none sons. Why I wondered, was she working in the fields all alone?

On the afternoon of the fourth day, as had become my habit, I began looking for Mrs. Bonachek as soon as I locked the school house door. When I couldn't find her, I felt a pang of guilty relief that I wouldn't have to see her that afternoon, call out a greeting that I knew she wouldn't return.

So I walked more boldly, dressing down Sears in language I could never put down on paper, enjoying the anarchy of my phrases even as I counted the blue crocus along the road.

Just as I came abreast of the row of stones that served to define the beginning of the Bonachek driveway, I saw her. She sat of the ground between the road and the small house, head bowed, arms folded across her chest. Her faded calico apron, its big seed pocket looking flat and empty, was spread on the ground beside her. She could have been sleeping, she was so still. I thought she might be sick, and would have gone to her, but she turned her head toward me, saw me, and shifted around until her hack was toward me.

I didn't stop. The road curved and after a while I couldn't see her without turning right around. I did look back once and saw Mrs. Bonachek upright again. She had left her apron on the ground, a faded-red bundle at the end of a furrow. She gathered up the skirt of her dress, filled it with seed grain, and continued her work. So primitive, I thought. How was it possible she had spawned the bright light that was Janos?

I found Martha in an extravagant mood when I reached home. The weather was frigid, but she, too, had seen the crocus. She announced that we would hold a tea to welcome spring. We would put on the tea frocks from her trunk and invite in some ladies from town. It would be a lark, she said, a coming out., I could invite anyone I wanted.

I still had Mrs. Bonachek on my mind. I couldn't help picturing her rising from her spat in the muddy fields to come sit on Martha's brocade sofa, so I said I would invite her first. The idea made us laugh until I had the hiccups. I said the woman had no daughters and probably needed some lively female company.

Martha went to the piano and banged out something suitable for a melodrama. I got a pan of hot water and soaked my cold feet while we talked about spring and the prospect of being warm again, truly warm, in all parts at once. I wondered what magazine ladies did at teas.

We were still planning little sandwiches and petit fours and onions cut into daisies when the doctor came in for supper. There were snowflakes on his beard and I saw snow falling outside, a lacy white curtain over the evening sky. When Martha looked away from the door, I saw tears in her eyes.

"You're late," Martha said to the doctor, managing a smile. "Out delivering Mrs. Bonachek?"

"No such luck." The doctor seemed grim. "I wish that just once the woman would call me in time. She delivered herself again. The baby died, low body temperature I suspect. A little girl. A pretty, perfect little girl."

I was stunned but I managed to blurt, "But she was working in the fields just this afternoon."

Martha and the doctor exchanged a glance that reminded me how much I still had to learn. Then the doctor launched into a speech about some people not having sense enough to take to their beds and what sort of life could a baby born into such circumstances expect anyway?

"The poor Dear," Martha said when he had run down. "She finally has a little girl to keep her company and it dies." She grabbed me by the arm. "We must go offer our consolation."

We put on our boots and coats and waited for the doctor to get his ancient Ford back out of the shed. It made a terrible racket, about which Martha complained gently, but there wasn't enough snow for the cutter. We were both disappointed — the cutter gave an occasion a certain weight.

"Say your piece then leave," the doctor warned as we rattled over the rutted road. "These are private people. They may not understand your intentions."

He didn't understand that Martha and I were suffering a bit of guilt from the fun we had at poor Mrs. Bonachek's expense. And we were bored. Barn sour, my mother would say. Tired of being cooped up all winter and in desperate need of some diversion.

We stormed the Bonachek's tiny clapboard house, our offers of consolation translated by a grim faced Janos. Martha was effusive. A baby girl should have a proper send-off, she said. There needed to be both a coffin and a dress. When was the funeral?

Mrs. Bonachek looked from me to Martha, a glaze over her mud-colored eyes. Janos shrugged his skinny shoulders. There was no money for funerals, he said. When a baby died, you called in the doctor for a death certificate then the county came for the remains. That was all.

Martha patted Mrs. Bonachek's scaly hands. Not to worry. We would take care of everything. And we did. Put off from our Spring Tea by the sudden change in the weather, we diverted our considerable social energy to the memorial services.

I found a nice wooden box of adequate size in the doctor's storeroom and painted it white. Martha went up the attic and brought down her beautiful pink silk gown and an old feather pillow. She didn't even wince and she ran her sewing shears up the delicate hand-turned seams. I wept. She hugged me and talked about God's will being done and Mrs. Bonachek's peasant strength. I was thinking about the spoiled dress.

We worked half the night. We padded the inside of the box with feathers and lined it with pink silk. We made a tiny dress and bonnet to match. The doctor had talked the county into letting us have a plot in the cemetery. It was such a little bit of ground, they couldn't refuse.

We contacted the parish priest, but he didn't want to perform the services. The county cemetery wasn't consecrated and he didn't know the Bonacheks. We only hoped it wasn't a rabbi that was needed because there wasn't one for miles. Martha reasoned that heaven was heaven and the Methodist preacher would have to do, since he was willing.

By the following afternoon everything was ready. The snow had turned to slush but our spirits weren't dampened. We set off, wearing prim navy blue because Martha said it was more appropriate for a child's funeral than somber black.

When the doctor drove us up to the small house, the entire Bonachek family, scrubbed and brushed, turned out to greet us.

Janos smiled for the first time I could remember. He fingered a frayed necktie that hung below his twine belt. He looked awkward, but I knew he felt elegant. Everyone, even Boya, wore some sort of shoes. It was a gala, if solemn event.

Mr. Bonachek, a scrawny, pale-faced man, relieved us of the makeshift coffin and led us into the single bedroom. The baby, wrapped in a scrap of calico, lay on the dresser. I unfolded the little silk dress on the bed while Martha shooed Mr. Bonachek out of the room.

"We should wash her," Martha said. A catch in her voice showed that her courage was failing. She began to unwrap the tiny creature. It was then I recognized the calico — Mrs. Bonachek's faded apron.

I thought of the nine sons lined up in the next room and Mrs. Bonachek sitting in the field with her apron spread on the cold ground beside her. Mrs. Bonachek who was so rich in sons.

I needed to know how many babies, how many girls, had died before this little one wrapped in the apron. Janos would tell me, Janos who had been so matter-of-fact about the routine business of death. I hadn't the courage at the moment to ask him.

Martha was working hard to maintain her composure. She had the baby dressed and gently laid her in the coffin. The baby was beautiful, her porcelain face framed in soft pink silk. I couldn't bear to see her in the box, like a shop-window doll.

I wanted to talk with Martha about the nagging suspicion that was taking shape in my mind. I hesitated too long.

Janos appeared at the door and I didn't want him to hear what I had to say. Actually, his face was so thin and expectant that it suddenly occurred to me that we hadn't brought any food for a proper wake.

"Janos," Martha whispered. "Tell your mother she may come in now."

Janos led his mother only as far as the threshold when she stopped stubbornly. I went to her, put my arm around her and impelled her to come closer to the coffin. When she resisted, I pushed. I was desperate to see some normal emotion from her. If she had none, what hope was there for Janos?

Finally, she shuddered and reached out a hand to touch the baby's cheek. She said something in her native language. I could understand neither the words nor the tone. It could have been a prayer, it could have been a curse.

When I let her go, she turned and looked at me. For the barest instant there was a flicker in her eyes that showed neither fear nor guilt about what I might have seen the afternoon before. I was disquieted because for the length of that small glimmer, she was beautiful. I saw who she might have become at another time, in a different place. When the tears at last came to my eyes, they were for her and not the baby.

Janos and Boya carried the coffin out to the bare front room and set it on the table. The preacher arrived and he gave his best two-dollar service even though there would be no payment. He spoke to the little group, the Bonacheks, Martha, the doctor and me, as if we were a full congregation. I don't remember what he said. I wasn't listening. I traced the pattern of the cheap, worn linoleum floor with my eyes and silently damned the poverty of the place and the cold that seeped in under the door.

We were a small, depressed-looking procession, walking down the muddy road to the county cemetery at the edge of town, singing along to hymns only the preacher seemed to know. At the gravesite, the preacher prayed for the sinless souls and the consigned her to the earth. It didn't seem to bother his that his principal mourners didn't understand a word he said.

Somehow, the doctor dissuaded Martha from inviting all of the Bonacheks home for supper — she, too, had belatedly thought about food.

As we walked back from the cemetery, I managed to separate the doctor from the group. I told him what was on my mind, what I had seen in the fields the day before. She had left her bundled apron at the end of a furrow and gone back to her work. I could not keep that guilty knowledge to myself.

The doctor wasn't as shocked as I expected him to be. But he was a man of worldly experience and I was merely a dairyman's daughter — the oldest child, the only girl in the family of five boys.

As the afternoon progressed, the air grew colder, threatening more snow. To this day, whenever I am very cold, I think of that afternoon. Janos, of course, fills that memory.

I think the little ceremony by strangers was sort of a coming out for him. He was suddenly not only a man of the community, but of the world beyond the road that ran between his farm and the school house, out where mountains and oceans were a possibility. It had been a revelation.

Janos called out to me and I stopped to wait for him, watching him run. He seemed incredibly small, outlined against the flat horizon. He was golden, and oddly ebullient.

Pale sunlight glinted off his bright head as he struggled through the slush on the road. Mud flew off his big boots in thick gobs and I thought his skinny legs would break with the weight of it. He seemed not to notice — mud was simply a part of the season's change, a harbinger of warmer days.

When he caught up, Janos was panting and red in the face. He looked like a wise old man for whom life held no secrets. As always, he held himself with a stiff dignity that I imagine suited him quite well when he was draped in his judge's robes.

Too breathless to speak, he placed in my had a fresh blue crocus he had plucked from the slush.

"Very pretty," I said, moved by his gesture. I looked into his smiling face and found courage. "What was the prayer your mother said for the baby?"

He shrugged and struggled for breath. Then he reached out and touched the delicate flower that was already turning brown from the warmth of my hand.

"No prayer," he said. "It's what she says. 'Know peace. Your sisters in heaven wait to embrace you.' "

I put my hand on his shoulder and looked up at the heavy, gathering clouds. "If it's snowing tomorrow," I said, "which books shall I bring?"

HIGH HEELS IN THE HEADLINER

"**E**xquisite prose, charming story. A nice read." Thea tossed the stack of reviews her editor had sent into the file drawer and slammed it shut. The reviews were always the same, exquisite, charming, nice. What she wanted to hear was, "Tough, gritty, compelling, real. Hardest of the hard-boiled."

Thea had honestly tried to break away from writing best-selling fluff. What she wanted more than anything was to be taken seriously as a writer among writers. To do that, she knew she had to achieve tough, gritty and real. The problem was, her whole damn life was exquisite, charming, nice.

Thea wrote from her own real-life experience, such as it was. One day, when she was about halfway through the first draft of *Lord Rimrock, L.A.P.D.*, a homeless man with one of those grubby cardboard signs — will work for food — jumped out at her from his spot on the median strip up on Pacific Coast Highway. Nearly scared her to death. She used that raw emotion, the fear like a cold dagger in her gut, to write a wonderful scene for Officer Lord Rimrock. But her editor scrapped it because it was out of tone with the rest of the book. Overdrawn, the editor said.

Fucking overdrawn, Thea muttered and walked up to the corner shop for a bottle of wine to take the edge off her *ennui*.

In her mind while she waited in line to pay, she rethought her detective. She chucked Lord Rimrock and replaced him with a Harvard man who preferred the action of big city police work to law school. He was tall and muscular with a streak of gray at the temples.

She was working on a name for him when she noticed that the man behind her in line had a detective shield hanging on his belt.

She gawked. Here in the flesh was a real detective, her first sighting. He was also a major a disappointment. His cheap suit needed pressing, he had a little paunch, and he was sweating. Lord Rimrock never sweated. Harvard men don't sweat.

"Excuse me," she said when he caught her staring.

"Don't worry about it." His worldly scowl changed to a smarmy smile and she realized that he had mistaken her curiosity for a come on. She went for it.

"What division do you work from?" That much she knew to ask.

"Homicide. Major crimes." *He smiled out of the side of his mouth, not giving up much, not telling her to go away either. She raised her beautiful eyes to meet his.* No. Beautiful was the wrong tone. Too charming.

"Must be interesting work," Thea said.

"Not very." *She knew he was flattered and played him like a ...* She'd work out the simile later.

"What you do is interesting to me," she said. "I write mystery novels."

"Oh yeah?" He was intrigued.

"I suppose you're always bothered by writers looking for help with procedural details."

"I never met a writer," he said. "Unless you count asshole reporters."

She laughed, scratching the Harvard man from her thoughts, dumping the gray streak at the temples. This detective had almost no hair at all.

Thea paid for her bottle of chardonnay. The detective put his six-pack on the counter, brushing her hand in passing. Before she could decide on an exit line, he said, "Have you ever been on a ride-along? You know, go out with the police and observe."

"I never have," she said. "It would be helpful. How does one arrange a ride-along?"

"I don't know any more." *The gravel in his voice told her he'd seen too much of life.* "Used to do it all the time. Damned liability shit now though, department has really pulled back. Too bad. I think what most taxpayers need is a dose of reality. If they saw what we deal with all day, they'd get off our backs."

Thea did actually raise her beautiful eyes to him. "I think the average person is fascinated by what you do. That's why they read mysteries. That's why I write them. I would love to sit down with you some time, talk about your experiences."

"Oh yeah?" He responded by pulling in his paunch. "I just finished up at a crime scene in the neighborhood. I'm on my way home. Maybe you'd like to go for a drink."

"Indeed, I would." Thea gripped the neck of the wine bottle, hesitating before she spoke. "Tell you what. If you take me by the crime scene and show me around, we can go to my place after, have some wine and discuss the details."

Bostitch was his name. He paid for his beer and took her out to his city car, awkward in his eagerness to get on with things.

The crime scene was a good one, an old lady stabbed in her bedroom. Bostitch walked Thea right into the apartment past the forensics people who were still sifting for evidence. He explained how the blood spatter patterns on the walls were like a map of the stabbing, showed her a long arterial spray. *On the carpet where the body was found, she could trace the contours of the woman's head and out-stretched arms. Like a snow angel made in blood.*

The victim's family arrived. They had come to look through the house to determine what, if anything, was missing, but all they could do was stand around, numbed by grief. Numbed? Was that it?

Thea walked up to the daughter and said, "How do you feel?"

"Oh, it's awful," the woman sobbed. "Mom was the sweetest woman on earth. Who would do this to her?"

Thea patted the daughter's back, her question still unanswered. How did she feel? Scorched, hollow, riven, shredded, iced in the gut? What?

"Seen enough?" Bostitch asked, taking Thea's arm.

She hadn't seen enough, but she smiled compliantly up into his face. She didn't want him to think she was a ghoul. Or a wimp. To her surprise, she was not bothered by the gore or the smell, or any of it. She was the totally objective observer, seeing everything through the eyes of her fictional detective character.

Bostitch showed her the homicide kit he kept in the trunk of his car, mostly forms, rubber gloves, plastic bags. She was more impressed by the name than the contents, but she took a copy of everything for future reference to make him happy.

By the time Bostitch drove her back to her house, Thea's detective had evolved. He was the son of alcoholics, grew up in Wilmington in the shadow of the oil refineries. He would have an ethnic name similar to Bostitch. The sort of man who wouldn't know where Harvard was.

In her exquisite living room, they drank the thirty-dollar chardonnay. Bostitch told stories, Thea listened. All the time she was smiling or laughing or pretending shock, she was making mental notes. *He sat with his arm draped on the back of the couch, the front of his jacket open, an invitation to come closer. He slugged down the fine wine like soda pop. When it was gone, he reached for the warm six-pack he had brought in with him and flipped one open.*

By that point, Bostitch was telling war stories about the old days when he was in uniform. The good old days. He had worked morning watch, the shift from midnight to seven. He liked being on patrol in the middle of the night because everything that went down at oh-dark-thirty had an edge. After work he and his partners would hit the early opening bars. They would get blasted and take women down to a cul-de-sac under the freeway and screw off the booze before they went home. Not beer, he told her. Hard stuff.

"Your girlfriend would meet you?" Thea asked.

"Girlfriend? Shit no. I'd never take a girlfriend down there. There are certain women who just wet themselves for a cop in uniform. We'd go, they'd show."

"I can't imagine," Thea said, wide-eyed, her worldly mien slipping. She couldn't imagine it. She had never had casual sex with anyone. Well, just once actually, with an English professor her freshman year. It had been pretty dull stuff and not worth counting.

"What sort of girls were they?" she asked him.

"All kinds. There was one — she was big, I mean big — we'd go pick her up on the way. She'd say, 'I won't do more than ten of you, and I won't take it in the rear.' She was a secretary or something."

"You made that up," Thea said.

"Swear to God," he said.

"I won't believe you unless you show me," Thea said. She knew where in the book she would use this gem, her raggedy old detective joining the young cowboys in uniform for one last blow out with young women. No. He'd have a young female partner and take her there to shock her. A rite of passage for a rookie female detective.

The problem was, Thea still couldn't visualize it, and she had to get it just right. She begged him, "Take me to this place."

She knew that Bostitch completely misunderstood that she was only interested for research purposes. Explaining this might not have gotten him up off the couch so fast. They stopped for another bottle on the way, a pint of scotch this time.

It was just dusk when Bostitch pulled up onto the hard-packed dirt of a vacant lot at the end of the cul-de-sac and parked. A small encampment of homeless people scurried away under the freeway when they recognized the city-issue car.

The cul-de-sac was at the end of a street to nowhere, a despoiled landscape of discarded furniture, cars and humanity. Even weeds couldn't thrive. She thought humanity wouldn't get past the editor — overdrawn — but that was the idea. She would find the right word later.

Bostitch skewed around in his seat to face her.

"We used to have bonfires here," he said. "Until the city got froggy about it. Screwed up traffic on the freeway. All the smoke."

"Spoiled your fun?" she said.

"It would take more than that." He smiled out the window. "One night, my partner talked me into coming out here before the shift was over. It wasn't even daylight yet. Some babe promised to meet him. I sat inside here and wrote reports while they did it on the hood. God, I'll never forget it. I'm working away in my seat with this naked white ass pumping against the windshield in front of my face — bump, bump, bump. Funny as hell. Bet that messed up freeway traffic."

Thea laughed, not at his story, but at her own prose version of it.

"You ever get naked on the hood of the car?" she asked. She'd had enough booze to ask it easily. For research.

"I like it inside better," he said.

"In the car?" she asked. She moved closer, *leaning near enough to smell the beer on his breath. During his twenty-five years with the police, he must have had half the women in the city. She wanted to know what they had taught him. What he might teach her.*

She lapped her tongue lightly along the inner curve of his lips. Thea said, with a throaty chuckle, "I won't do more than ten of you. And I won't take it in the rear."

When he took her in his arms he wasn't as rough as she had hoped he would be. She set the pace by the eager, almost violent way she tore loose his tie, ripped open his shirt. His five-o'clock shadow sanded a layer of skin off her chin.

They ended up in the back seat, their clothes as wrinkled and shredded as the crime scene report under them. At the moment of her ecstasy the heel of Thea's shoe thrust up through the velour headliner. She looked at the long tear. *The sound of the rip was like cymbals crashing at the peak of a symphony, except the only music was the rhythmic grunting and groaning from the tangle of bodies in the backseat. She jammed her foot through the hole, bracing it against the hard metal roof of the car to get some leverage to meet his thrusting, giving him a more solid base to bang against.*

Bostitch seemed to stop breathing altogether. His face grew a dangerous red and drew up into an agonized sort of grimace that stretched every sinew in his neck. Thea was beginning to worry that she might have killed him when he finally exhaled.

"Oh Jesus," he moaned. "Oh sweet, sweet Jesus."

She untangled her foot from the torn headliner and wrapped her bare legs around him, trapping him inside her until the pulsing ceased. Maybe not, she thought. Pulsing, throbbing were definitely over used.

After the afterglow, what would she feel? Not shame or anything akin to it. She smiled; pride in her prowess. She had whipped his ass and left him gasping. Thea buried her face against his chest and bit his small hard nipple.

"You're amazing," he said, still breathing hard.

She said nothing. That moment was definitely not the time to explain that it was her female detective, Ricky or maybe Marty Tenwolde, who was amazing. Thea herself was far too inhibited to have initiated the wild sex that had left their automobile nest in serious need of repair.

When they had pulled their clothes back together, he said, "Now what?"

"Skid Row," she said. "I've always been afraid to go down there, but I need to see it for the book I'm working on."

"Good reason to be afraid." *The cop spoke with a different voice than the lover, a deep, weary growl that* something or other. "You don't really want to go down there."

"I do, though. With you. You're armed. You're the law. We'll be safe."

She batted her big beautiful eyes again. Flattery and some purring were enough to sway him. He drove her downtown to Skid Row.

Thea had never seen anything as squalid and depraved. Toothless, stoned hookers running down the middle of the street. Men dry heaving in the gutter. *The smell alone made him wish she hadn't come along. He was embarrassed that she saw the old wino defecate openly on the sidewalk. But she only smiled that wry smile that always made the front of his slacks feel tight.*

There was a six or seven person brawl in progress on one corner. Thea loved it when Bostitch merely honked his horn to make them scatter like so many cockroaches.

"Seen enough?" he asked.

"Yes. Thank you."

Bostitch held her hand all the way back to her house.

"Will you come in?" she asked him.

"I'll come in. But don't expect much more out of my sorry old carcass. I haven't been that fired up since ..."

"I thought for a minute you had died," she said. "I didn't know where to send the body."

"Felt like I was on my way to heaven." He slid a business card with a gold detective shield from behind his visor and handed it to her. "You ever need anything, page me through the office."

So, he had a wife. A lot of men do. Thea hadn't considered a wife in the equation. She liked it, nice characterization. Bostitch called home from the phone on Thea's desk and told the wife he'd be out late on a case. Maybe all night.

"No wonder you fool around," Thea said when he turned his attention back to her. "It's too easy. Does your wife believe you?"

He shrugged. "She doesn't much bother anymore believing or not believing."

"Good line," Thea said. More than anything, she wanted to turn on her computer and get some of what she had learned on disk before she forgot anything. She had a whole new vocabulary: boot the door meant to kick it down, elwopp was life without possibility of parole, fifty-one-fifty was a mental incompetent. So many things to catalogue.

"Where's your favorite place to make love?" she asked him.

"In a bed."

That's where they did it next. At least, that's where they began. Bostitch was stunned, pleased, by the performance Thea coaxed from him. He gave Thea a whole chapter.

All the next week she was his shadow. She stood beside him during the autopsy of the stabbing victim, professional and detached because female detective Marty Tenwolde would be. The top of the old lady's skull made a pop like a champagne cork when the coroner sawed it off, but she didn't even startle. She was as tough and gritty as any man on the force. She was tender, too. After a long day of detecting, she took the old guy home and screwed him until he begged for mercy. Detective Tenwolde felt ...

That feeling stuff was the hard part. Tenwolde would feel attached to her old married partner. Be intrigued by him. She couldn't help mothering him a bit, but she could by no stretch describe her feelings as maternal. Love was going too far.

Thea watched Bostitch testify in court one day. A murder case, but not a particularly interesting one. It was a garden variety family shootout, drunk husband takes after estranged wife and her boyfriend. Thea added to her new vocabulary, learning that dead bang meant a case with an almost guaranteed conviction.

Bostitch looked sharper than usual and Thea was impressed by his professionalism. Of course, he winked at her when he thought the jury wasn't looking, checked for her reaction whenever he scored a point against the defense attorney. She always smiled back at him, but she was really more interested in the defendant, a pathetic little man who professed profound grief when he took the stand in his defense. He cried. *Without his wife, he was only a shell occupying space in this universe. His wife had defined his existence, made him complete. Killing her had only been a crude way to kill himself.* If he had any style, he would beg for the death sentence and let the state finish the job for him. Thea wondered what it felt like to lose a loved one in such a violent fashion.

Detective Tenwolde cradled her partner's bleeding head in her lap, knowing he was dying. She pressed her face close to his ear and whispered, "My only regret is I'll never be able to fuck you again, big guy. I love your ragged old ass." Needed something, but it was a good farewell line. Tough, gritty, yet tender.

Out in the corridor after court, the deputy district attorney complimented Bostitch's testimony. Thea, holding his hand, felt proud. No, she thought, she felt lustful. *If he had asked her to, for his reward in getting the kid convicted, she would gladly have blown Bostitch right there on the escalator.* Maybe she did love him. Something to think about.

After court, Thea talked Bostitch into taking her to a Hungarian restaurant he had told her about. He had had a run in with a lunatic there a year or so earlier. Shot the man dead. Thea wanted to see where.

"There's nothing to see," he said as he pulled into the hillside parking lot. "But the food's okay. Mostly goulash. You know, like stew. We might as well eat."

They walked inside with their arms around each other. The owner knew Bostitch and showed them to a quiet booth in a far back corner. It was very dark.

"I haven't seen Laszlo's brother for four or five months," the owner said, setting big plates of steaming goulash in front of them. He had a slight accent. "He was plenty mad at you, Bostitch, I tell you. Everybody knows Laszlo was a crazy man, always carrying those guns around. What could you do but shoot him? He shot first. I think maybe his brother is a little nuts, too."

"Show me where he died," Thea said, her lips against Bostitch's jug-like ear. He turned his face to her and kissed her.

"Let's eat and get out of here," he said. "We shouldn't have come."

There was a sudden commotion at the door and a big, fiery-eyed man burst in. The first thing Thea noticed was the shotgun he held at his side. The owner rushed up to him, distracted his attention away from Thea's side of the restaurant.

"Shh, Thea." Bostitch, keeping his eyes on the man with the shotgun, pulled his automatic from his belt holster. "That's Laszlo's brother. Someone must have called him, told him I was here. We're going to slip out the back way while they have him distracted."

"But he has a gun. He'll shoot someone."

"No he won't. He's looking for me. Once I'm out of here, they'll calm him down. Let me get out the door, then you follow me.

Whatever you do, don't get close to me, and for chrissake stay quiet. Don't attract his attention." Bostitch slipped out of the booth.

She felt *alive. Adrenaline wakened every primitive instinct for survival. Every instinct to protect her man. If the asshole with the gun made so much as a move toward Bostitch, Tenwolde would grind him into dogmeat. Bostitch was only one step from safety when Tenwolde saw the gunman turn and spot him.*

Dogmeat was good, Thea thought. The rest she was still unclear about. That's when she stood up and screamed, "Don't shoot him. I love him."

Bostitch would have made it out the door, but Thea's outburst caused him to look back. That instant's pause was just long enough for the befuddled gunman to find Bostitch in his sights and fire a double-aught load into his abdomen. Bostitch managed to fire off a round of his own. The gunman was dead before he fell.

Thea ran to Bostitch and caught him as he slid to the floor, leaving a wide red smear on the wall.

His head was heavy in her arms.

"Why?" he sighed. His eyes went dull.

Tenwolde watched the light fade from her partner's eyes, felt his last breath escape from his shattered chest. She couldn't let him see her cry; he'd tease her forever. That's when she lost it. Bostitch had used up his forever.

"It's not fair, big guy," *she said, smoothing his sparse hair. She felt a hole open in her chest as big as the gaping wound through his. Without him, she was incomplete.* "You promised me one more academy-award fuck. You're not going back on your promise, are you?"

He was gone. Still, she held on to him, her cheek against his, his blood on her lips. "I never told you, Bostitch. I love your raggedy old ass."

WENDY GOES TO THE MORGUE

There is a big difference between writing a tough, graphic murder scene, and seeing the product of the real thing up close.

I was working on *Telling Lies* (Dutton 1992, Onyx 1993), the first in my mystery series with filmmaker Maggie MacGowen. At one point in the story, Maggie has to go to the Los Angeles County morgue to look at a body. For the book, for you, I wanted to get it right both visually and emotionally. I had to go to the morgue.

The first thing you need to know is, Maggie is a lot tougher and braver than I am. "Soft-spoken, genteel college professor" was how National Public Radio introduced me recently. As much as I hate that description, it really is not far off the mark (but I'm working on it).

So, one smoggy summer day my consultant on things police, Detective Dennis Payne, LAPD Robbery-Homicide Division, called and said he had to go the morgue to pick up some "property" (don't ask). Did I want to come along? I dredged up sufficient bravado, and went.

In the first place, the L.A. morgue is nothing like the TV show, *Quincy*. No shiny stainless, no view windows or sleek offices. The real thing is housed in a square, dull-gray, four or five story building on the downslope corner of the massive L.A. County-USC Hospital Medical Center grounds. The surrounding neighborhood is wrecking yards, the Lincoln Heights Jail, railroad switching yards, a couple of freeways, a McDonald's and a Holiday Inn that needs some paint.

While he parked his city-issue car — the only green four door in a lot full of government mud-brown Chevys (that's California mud-brown) — Detective Payne gave me some tips:

42

The morgue isn't tidy. When the door opens, what you see is bodies, everyone in the county who dies under questionable circumstances. First thing when you go inside, he said, is take a deep breath, get used to the smell in a hurry.

He also warned me not to touch anything. No problem there.

"It's not like the movies," he said, "not sheet-covered bodies with toe tags sticking out."

"No toe tags?" I asked.

"No sheets," he said.

Forewarned is forearmed, right?

Dennis opened the big door, I took a handful of his tweed upholstered elbow, and drew in my deep breath. A big mistake; the death smell is like nothing else. It is sweet and heavy and settles inside your lungs. The smell is so pervasive that pretty soon you taste it every time you exhale.

The long hallway inside the morgue is little more than four gurneys wide, with occupied gurneys lined up along the sides sometimes two and three deep. The dead aren't laid out with hands neatly folded on their chests. Tumbled out comes closer.

Except for Dennis's shoulder ahead of me, there was no place I could look without seeing the violently dead. I took it in small snaps, focusing on the wholish parts of those we passed. When Dennis turned to check on me, I smiled — even the genteel and soft-spoken can lie with their faces. I was feeling about stage-two panicky, but I didn't want him to know it, decide I was a wimp and then not invite me along on other adventures. He didn't seem affected by the place. Old hat for him: Homicide detectives routinely attend the autopsies related to their cases.

Dennis stopped to show me an especially nice example of a gunshot entrance wound. He very thoroughly explained the characteristic cruciform tearing in the flesh, demonstrated how to find the direction of entry from the pattern of bruising. It was fascinating as long as I focused on the wounds and not on the man lying there, looking back at me.

The bodies in the hall were waiting their turns at one of the two big autopsy rooms where about six bodies can be processed at once. The autopsy rooms, in contrast to the hall, are brightly lit and full of activity. Again, there is no clinical gleam. The standard tools are garden shears and soup ladles. Don't call and ask me about it. In *Telling Lies* Maggie goes into the details for me. She handled the entire experience better than I did. I will tell you this, though. After an autopsy your victim can't be dressed in decoulletage for the funeral. A generous technician may give the dearly departed a face lift when he pulls the face back up over the skull when the cadaver is reassembled.

I had difficulty with faces, but I managed to hang in without disgracing myself, or Dennis. Until we passed a corpse with no face at all. When I realized what I was looking at, I said to hell with bravado, gripped Dennis's arm in another place and seriously studied the weave of his tweed jacket. Nice jacket. Next time I hope he wears plaid.

By the time we got to the X-Ray room, I had all that I needed for Maggie's trip to the morgue. All five senses were certainly covered (when the top of the skull is removed, it pops like a champagne cork). I had the emotional stuff in hand, too. True to form, though her stomach gave one leap, Maggie was a brick at the morgue. She even managed to speak coherently.

I love hanging out with Maggie. Since the morgue, we have seen Skid Row late at night, federal housing projects on payday, the police academy bar, the lockup at Parker Center, figured out DNA and blood-spatter patterns, watched women officers boxing, heard the talk and walked the walk. Next to royalty checks, doing practical research is far and away the most fun aspect of writing crime fiction. Another time, I'll tell you what I did for *Midnight Baby*, Maggie's second adventure. It was certainly more fun than the morgue. Trust me.

One last thing. You know what Detective Payne said to me as we emerged from the morgue and out into the L.A. smog again?

"So, shall we get lunch?"

NEW MOON AND RATTLESNAKES
A California Short Story

Lise caught a ride at a truck stop near Riverside, in a big rig headed for Phoenix. The driver was a paunchy, lonely old geek whose come-on line was a fatherly routine. She helped him play his line because it got her inside the air-conditioned cab of his truck and headed east way ahead of her schedule.

"Sweet young thing like you shouldn't be thumbing rides," he said, helping Lise with her seatbelt. "Desert can be awful damn dangerous in the summertime."

"I know the desert. Besides ..." She put her hand over his hairy paw. "I'm not so young and there's nothing sweet about me."

He laughed, but he looked at her more closely. Looked at the heavy purse she carried with her, too. After that long look, he dropped the fatherly routine. She was glad, because she didn't have a lot of time to waste on preliminaries.

The tired old jokes he told her got steadily gamier as he drove east out Interstate 60. Cheap new housing tracts and pink stucco malls gave way to a landscape of razor-sharp yucca and shimmering heat, and all the way Lise laughed at his stupid jokes only to let him know she was hanging in with him.

Up the steep grade through Banning, and Beaumont, and Cabazon she laughed on cue, watching him go through his gears, deciding whether she could drive the truck without him. Or not. Twice, to speed things along, she told him jokes that made his bald head blush flame red.

Before the Palm Springs turn-off, he suggested they stop at an Indian Bingo palace for cold drinks and a couple of games. Somehow,

NEW MOON AND RATTLESNAKES

Before the Palm Springs turn-off, he suggested they stop at an Indian Bingo palace for cold drinks and a couple of games. Somehow, while she was distracted watching how the place operated, his hand kept finding its way into the back of her Spandex tank top.

The feel of him so close, his suggestive leers, the smell of him, the smoky smell of the place, made her clammy all over. But she kept up a good front, didn't retch when her stomach churned. She had practice; for five years she had kept up a good front, and survived because of it. Come ten o'clock, she encouraged herself, there would be a whole new order of things.

After bingo, it was an hour of front-seat wrestling, straight down the highway to a Motel 6 — all rooms $29.95, cable TV and a phone in every room. He told her what he wanted; she asked him to take a shower first.

In Riverside, he'd said his name was Jack. But the name on the Louisiana driver's license she found in his wallet said Henry LeBeau. He was in the shower, singing, when she made this discovery. Lise practiced writing the name a couple of times on motel stationery while she placed a call on the room phone. Mrs. Henry LeBeau, Lise LeBeau, she wrote it until the call was answered.

"I'm out," Lise said.

"You're lying."

"Not me," she said. "Penalty for lying's too high."

"I left my best man at the house with you. He would have called me."

"If he could. Maybe your best man isn't as good as you thought he was. Maybe I'm better."

Waiting for more response from the other end, she wrote LeBeau's name a few more times, wrote it until it felt natural to her hand.

Finally, she got more than heavy breathing from the phone. "Where are you, Lise?"

"I'm a long way into somewhere else. Don't bother to go looking, because this time you won't find me."

"Of course I will."

She hung up.

Jack/Henry turned off the shower. Before he was out of the bathroom, fresh and clean and looking for love, Lise was out of the motel and down the road. With his wallet in her bag.

The heat outside was like a frontal assault after the cool, dim room; hundred and ten degrees, zero percent humidity according to a sign. Afternoon sun slanted directly into Lise's eyes and the air smelled like truck fuel and hot pavement, but it was better than the two-day sweat that had filled the big-rig cab, that had followed them into the motel. She needed a dozen hot breaths to get his stench out of her.

The motel wasn't in a place, nothing but a graded spot at the end of a freeway offramp halfway between Los Angeles and Phoenix; a couple of service stations and a mini-mart, a hundred miles of scrubby cactus and sharp rocks for neighbors. Shielding her eyes, Lise quick-walked toward the freeway, looking for possibilities even before she crossed the road to the Texaco station.

The meeting she needed to attend would be held in Palm Springs and she had to find a way to get there. She knew for a dead certainty she didn't want to get into another truck, and she couldn't stay in the open.

Heat blazed down from the sky, bounced up off the pavement and caught her both ways. Lise began to panic. Fifteen minutes, maybe twenty, under the sun and she knew she would be fried. But it wasn't the heat that made her run for the shelter of the covered service station. After being confined for so long, open space sometimes frightened her.

The Texaco and its mini-mart were busy with a transient olio show: Cranky families in vans, chubby truckers, city smoothies in desert vacation togs and too much shiny jewelry, everyone in a hurry to fill up, scrape the bugs off the windshield, and get back on the road with the air-conditioning buffering them from the relentless heat.

As she walked past the pumps, waiting for opportunity to present itself, an old white-haired guy in a big new Cadillac slid past her and pulled up next to the mini-mart. He was a very clean-looking man, the sort, she thought, who doesn't like to get hot and mussed. Like her husband. When he got out of his car to go into the mini-mart, the creampuff left his engine running and his air-conditioner blowing to keep the car's interior cool.

Lise saw the man inside the store, spinning a rack of road maps, as she got into his car and drove away.

When she hit the on-ramp, backtracking west, Mr. Henry LeBeau, half-dressed and sweating like a come-back wrestler, was standing out in front of the motel, looking upset, looking around like he'd lost something.

"Goodbye, Mr. LeBeau." Lise smiled at his tiny figure receding in her rearview mirror. "Thanks for the ride." Then she looked all around, half-expecting to spot a tail, to find a fleet of long, shiny black cars deployed to find her, surround her, take her back home; escape couldn't be this easy. But the only shine she saw came from mirages, like silver puddles splashed across the freeway. She relaxed some, settled against the leather upholstery, aimed the air vents on her face and changed the Caddie's radio station from a hundred violins to Chopin.

Her transformation from truck-stop dolly to mall matron took less than five minutes. She wiped off the heavy make-up she had acquired in Riverside, covered the skimpy tank top with a blouse from her bag, rolled down the cuffs of her denim shorts to cover three-more inches of her muscular thighs, traded the hand-tooled boots for graceful leather sandals, and tied her windblown hair into a neat ponytail at the back of her neck. When she checked her face in the mirror, she saw any lady in a check-out line looking back at her.

Lise took the Bob Hope Drive offramp, sighed happily as the scorched and barren virgin desert gave way to deep green golf courses, piles of shi-shi condos, palm trees, fountains, and posh restaurants whose parking lots were garnished with Jags, Caddies and Benzes.

She pulled into one of those lots and, with the motor running, took some time to really look over what she had to work with. American Express Card signed H.G. LeBeau. MasterCard signed Henry LeBeau. Four hundred in cash. The wallet also had some gas company cards, two old condoms, a picture of an ugly wife, and a slip of paper with a four-digit number. Bless his heart, she thought, smiling, Henry had given her a PIN number, contributed to her range of possibilities.

Lise committed the four digits to memory, put the credit cards and cash into her pocket, then got out into the blasting heat to stuff the wallet into a trash can before she drove on to the Palm Desert Mall.

Like a good Scout, Lise left the Caddie in the mall parking lot just as she had found it, motor running, doors unlocked, keys inside. Without a backward glance, she headed straight for I. Magnin. Wardrobe essentials and a beautiful leather and brocade suitcase to carry it consumed little more than an hour. She signed for purchases alternately as Mrs. Henry LeBeau or H.G. LeBeau as she alternated the credit cards. She felt safe doing it; in Magnin's, no one ever dared ask for I.D.

Time was a problem, and so was cash enough to carry through the next few days, until she could safely use other resources.

As soon as Henry got himself pulled together, she knew he would report his cards lost. She also knew he wouldn't have the balls to confess the circumstances under which the cards got away from him, so she wasn't worried about the police. But, once the cards were reported they would be useless. How long would it take him, she wondered?

From a teller machine, she pulled the two-hundred dollar cash advance limit off the MasterCard, then used the card a last time to place another call.

"You're worried," she said into the receiver. "You have that meeting tonight and I have distracted you. You have a problem, because if I'm not around to sign the final papers, everything falls apart. Now you're caught in a double bind: you can't stand up the Congressman and you can't let me get away, and you sure as hell can't be in two places at once. What are you going to do?"

"This is insane." The old fury was in his voice this time. "Where are you?"

"Don't leave the house. Don't even think about it. I'll know if you do. I'll see the lie in your eyes. I'll smell it on every lying word that comes out of your mouth." It was easy; the words just came, like playing back an old, familiar tape. The words did sound funny to her, though, coming out of her own mouth. She wondered how he came up with such garbage, and, more to the point, how he had persuaded her over the years that death could be any worse than living under his dirty thumb.

The true joy of talking to him over the telephone was having the power to turn him off. She hung up, took a deep breath, blew out the sound of him.

In the soft soil of a planter next to the phone bank, she dug a little grave for the credit card and covered it over.

After a late lunch, accompanied by half a bottle of very cold champagne, Lise had her hair done, darkened back to its original color and cut very short. The beauty parlor receptionist was accommodating, added a hundred dollars to the American Express bill and gave Lise the difference in cash.

Lise had been moderately surprised when the card flew through clearance, but risked using it one last time. From a gourmet boutique, she picked up some essentials of another kind: a few bottles of good wine, a basket of fruit, a variety of expensive little snacks. On her way out of the store, she jettisoned the American Express into a bin of green jelly beans.

Every transaction fed her confidence, assured her she had the courage to go through with the plan that would set her free forever. By the time she had finished her chores, her accumulation of bags was almost more than she could carry, and she was exhausted. Still, she felt better than she had for a very long time.

When she headed for the mall exit on the far side from where she had left Mr. Clean's Cadillac, Lise was not at all sure what would happen next. She still had presentiments of doom, she still looked over her shoulder and in reflections of the crowd in every window she passed. Logic said she was safe, conditioning kept her wary, kept her moving.

Highjacking a car with its motor running had worked so well once, she decided to try it again. She had any number of prospects to choose from. The mall's indoor ice skating rink — so bizarre, the rink overlooked a giant cactus garden — and the movie theater complex next to it, meant parents waiting at the curb for kids. Among that row of cars, Lise counted three with motors running, air-conditioning purring, and no drivers in sight.

Lise considered her choices: a Volvo station wagon, a small Beemer, and a teal-blue Jag. She ran through "eeny, meeny," though she had targeted the Jag right off; the Jag was the first car in the row.

Bags in the backseat, Lise in the driver's seat and pulling away from the curb before she had the door all the way shut. After a stop on a side street to pack her new things into the suitcase, she drove straight to the Palm Springs airport. She left the Jag in a passenger loading zone and, bags in hand, rushed into the terminal like a tourist late for a flight.

She stopped at the first phone.

"You've checked, haven't you?" she said when he picked up. "You sent your goons to look in on me. You know I'm out. We're so close, I know everything you've done. I can hear your thoughts running through my head. You're thinking the deal is dead without me. And I'm in another time zone."

"You won't get away from me."

"I think you're angry. If I don't correct you when you have bad thoughts, you'll ruin everything."

"Stop it."

She looked at her nails, kept her voice flat. "You're everything to me. I'd kill you before I let you go."

"Please, Lise." His voice had a catch, almost like a sob when she hung up.

She left the terminal by a different door, came out at the cab stand, where a single cab waited. The driver looked like a cousin of the Indians at the Bingo palace, and, because of the nature of the meeting scheduled that night, she hesitated. In the end, she handed the cabbie her suitcase and gave him the address of a hotel in downtown Palm Springs, an address she had memorized a long time ago.

"Pretty dead over there," the driver said, fingering the leather grips of her bag. "Hard to get around without a car when you're so far out. I can steer you to nicer places closer in. Good rates off season, too."

"No, thank you," she said.

He talked the entire way. He asked more questions than she answered, and made her feel uneasy. Why should a stranger need to know so much? Could the driver possibly be a plant sent to bring her back? Was the conversation normal chit chat? That last question bothered her: she had been cut off for so long, would she know normal if she met it head on?

When the driver dropped her at a funky old place on the block behind the main street through Palm Springs, she was still wary. She waited until he was gone before she picked up her bag and walked inside.

Off season, the hotel felt empty. The manager was old enough to be her mother; a desert woman with skin like a lizard and tiny black eyes.

"I need a room for two nights," Lise told her.

The manager handed her a registration card. "Put it on a credit card or cash in advance?"

Lise paid cash for the two nights, and gave the woman a fifty dollar deposit for the use of the telephone.

"It's quiet here," the manager said, handing over a key. "Too hot this time of year for most people."

"Quiet is what I'm counting on," Lise said. "I'm not expecting any calls, but if someone asks for me, I'd appreciate it if you never heard of me."

When the manager smiled, her black eyes nearly disappeared among the folds of dry skin. "Man trouble, honey?"

"Is there another kind?"

"From my experience, it's always either a man or money. And from the look of you," the manager said, glancing at the suitcase and the gourmet shop's handled bag, "I'd put my nickel on the former. Don't worry, honey, I didn't get a good look at you and I already forgot your name."

The name Lise wrote on the registration card was the name on a bottle of chardonnay in her bag: Rutherford Hill.

The hotel was built like an old adobe ranch house, with thick walls and rounded corners, Mexican tile on the floors, dark, open-beamed ceilings. Lise's room was a bit threadbare, but it was larger, cleaner, nicer than she had expected for the price. The air-conditioner worked and there was a kitchenette with a little, groaning refrigerator for her wine. For the first time in five years, she had her own key, and used it to bolt the door on the inside.

From her tiny balcony Lise could see both the pool in the patio below and the rocky base of Mount San Jacinto a quarter mile away. Already the sun had slipped behind the crest of the mountain, leaving the hotel in blue shade. Finally, Lise was able to smell the real desert, dry sage and blooming oleander, air without exhaust fumes.

A gentle breeze blew in off the mountain. Lise left the window open and lay down on the bed to rest for just a moment. When she opened her eyes again, floating on the cusp between sleep and wakefulness, the room was washed in soft lavender light — hot, but fragrant with the flowers on the patio below. She could hear a fountain somewhere, now and then voices at a distance. For the first time in a long time, she didn't go straight to the door and listen for breathing on the other side.

Lise slipped into the new swimsuit — a little snug in the rear, she hadn't taken time to try it on before she bought it. She needed the ice pick she found on the sink to pry out the ice trays so she could fill the paper ice bucket. She liked the heavy feel of the ice pick. While she opened a bottle of wine and cut some fruit and cheese, she made a call.

"Sunset will be exactly 8:32. No moon tonight. Rattlesnakes love a moonless night. You better stay indoors or you might get bitten."

"What is your game?"

"Your game. I'm a quick learner. Remember when you said that? I think I have all your moves down. Let's see how they play."

"You're a rookie, Lise. You won't make it in the big leagues. And every game I play, baby, is the big one." He'd had some time to get over the initial surprise and anger, so he was back on the offensive. He scared her, but because he couldn't touch her, her resolve held firm as she listened to him. "You'll be back, Lise. You'll take a few hard ones to the head and realize how cold and cruel that world out there is. You'll beg me to take you in and watch over you again. You can be mad at me all you want, but it isn't my fault you're such a princess you can't find your way across the street alone. Blame your asshole father for spoiling you. If it wasn't for me ..."

"If it wasn't for you, my father would be alive," she said, cutting off his windup. "I have the proof with me."

The moment of silence told her she had hit home. She hung up.

Lise swam in the small pool until she felt clean again, until the heat and the sweat and the layer of fine sand had all been washed away, until the warm, chlorinated water had bleached away the fevered touch of Henry LeBeau. Some of her new hair color was bleached away, too; it left a shadow on the towel when she got out and dried off.

Lise poured a bathroom tumbler full of straw-colored wine and stretched out on a chaise beside the pool. There was still some blue in the sky when the manager came out to switch on the pool lights.

"Sure was a hot one." The manager nursed a drink of her own. "Course, till October they're pretty much all hot ones. Let me know when you're finished with the pool. Sun heats it up so much that every night I let out some of the warm water and replace it with cold. Otherwise I'll have parboiled guests on my hands."

"How many guests are in the hotel?" Lise asked.

"Just you, honey." The manager drained her glass. "One guest is one more than I had all last week."

Lise offered her the tray of cheese. "Can you sit down for a minute? Have a little happy hour with the registered guests."

"I don't mind." The manager pulled up a chaise next to Lise and let Lise fill her empty glass with chardonnay. "I have to say, off season it does get lonely now and then. We used to close up from Memorial

Day to Labor Day — the whole town did. We're more year 'round now. Hell, there's talk we'll have casino gambling soon and become the new Vegas."

"Vegas is noisy."

"Vegas is full of crooks." The manager nibbled some cheese. "I wouldn't mind having my rooms booked up again. But the high-rollers would stay in the big new hotels and I'd get their hookers and pushers. Who needs that?"

Lise sipped from her glass and stayed quiet. The manager sighed as she looked up into the darkening sky. "Was a time when this place hopped with Hollywood people and their carryings on. Liberace and a bunch of them had places just up the road here, you know. We used to get the overflow, and were they ever a wild crowd. I miss them. That set has moved on east, fancier places like Palm Desert. I still get an old-timer now and then, but most of my guests are Canadian snowbirds. They start showing up around Thanksgiving, spend the winter. Nice bunch, but awful tame." She winked at Lise. "Tame, but easier to deal with than Vegas hookers."

"I'm sure," Lise said.

With a thoughtful tilt to her head, the manager looked again, and more closely, at Lise. "I'm pretty far off the beaten track. How'd you ever find my place?"

"I passed the hotel when I was up here visiting. It seemed so ..." Lise refilled their glasses. "It seemed peaceful."

Lise could feel the manager's shiny black eyes on her. "You okay, honey?"

Lise held up the empty bottle. "I'm getting there."

"That kind of medicine is only going to last so long. It's none of my business, but you want to talk about it?"

"I'm sure you've heard it all before. Long-suffering wife skips out on asshole husband."

"I've not only heard it, I've lived it. Twice." The manager put her weathered hand on Lise's bare knee and smiled sweetly. "You're going to be fine. Just give it some time."

The wine, fatigue, the sweet concern on the old woman's face all in combination, Lise felt the cracks inside open up and let in some light. The last time anyone had shown her genuine concern had been five years ago, when her father was still alive. There was five years accumulation of moss on her father's marble headstone. Lise began to cry softly.

The manager pulled a packet of tissue out of her pocket. "Atta girl. Let the river flow."

Lise laughed then.

"Does he know where you are?"

Lise shook her head. "Not yet."

"Not yet?"

"Given time, he'll find me. He always does. No matter how far I run, he can find me. He's a powerful man with powerful friends."

"What are you going to do?"

Lise shrugged, though she knew very well. The answer was in the bag upstairs in the closet.

"Well, don't you worry, honey. No one knows about this old place. And I already told you, I don't remember what you look like and I don't recall your name." The manager picked up the empty bottle and looked at the Rutherford Hill label with sly humor folding the corners of her creased face. "Though, come to think of it, the name does have a familiar ring."

The sun set at exactly 8:32. Lise showered and changed into long khakis and a pale peach shirt, both in tones of the desert floor. She took her bag out of the closet and held it on her lap while she waited for the last reflected light of the day to fade.

NEW MOON AND RATTLESNAKES

The big story on the local TV news was what the manager had been talking about, the growing controversy over the proposal to build a Vegas-style casino on Tahquitz Indian tribal land at the southern city limits of Palm Springs. A congressional delegation had come to town to investigate. As the video-taped congressmen, wearing sober gray and big smiles, paraded across the barren, hillside site, Lise felt chilled; her husband, wearing his own big smile, was among the entourage. She knew why he was in town and who he would be meeting with. But she hadn't expected to see him before ...

She pulled the bag closer against her and checked the clock beside the bed. If the clock was correct, he had nearly run out of time.

When Lise walked downstairs, she could see the flickering light of a television behind the front desk, could hear the manager moving around and further coverage of the big story spieling across the empty lobby. Quietly, Lise went out through the patio, the bag hanging heavily from her shoulder.

Maybe rattlesnakes do like a moonless night, she thought. But they hate people and slither away pretty fast. Lise walked along a sandy path that paralleled the road, feeling the stored heat in the earth soak through her sneakers. Palms rustled overhead like the rattle of a snake and set her on edge.

Lise slipped on a pair of surgical gloves, and being excruciatingly careful not to disturb the beautiful, five-year-old set of prints on the barrel, took the .380 out of her bag, pumped a round into the chamber in case of emergency, and walked on.

The house where the meeting would take place had belonged to her father. Before her marriage, she used to drive out on weekends and school vacations to visit him. After her marriage, after her father's funeral, her husband had taken the place over to use when he had deals to make in the desert. Now and then, when he couldn't make other arrangements for her, Lise had come along. It had been during a recent weekend, when she was banished to the bedroom during a business meeting, that Lise had figured out a way to get free of him. Forever.

The house sat in a shallow box canyon at the end of the same street the hotel was on. Her father had built the house in the Spanish style, a long string of rooms that all opened onto a central patio. Like the hotel, the walls were thick to keep out the worst of the heat. And like the hotel, like a fort, it was very quiet.

All of the lights were on. Lise knew that for a meeting this delicate, there would be no entourage. Inside the house, there would be only three people: the non-English speaking housekeeper, Lise's husband and the Congressman. She knew the routine well; the Congressman was as much a part of her husband's inheritance from her father as Lise and the house were.

Outside, there was a guard on the front door, and one on the back patio, standing away from the windows so that his presence wouldn't offend the Congressman. Both of the guards were big and ugly, snakes of another kind, and more intimidating than they were smart. By circling wide, Lise got past the man in front, made it to the edge of the patio before she was seen. It wasn't the hired muscle who spotted her first.

Luther, her father's old rottweiler guard dog, ambled across the patio to greet Lise. She pushed his head aside to keep him from muzzling her crotch, made him settle for a head scratch.

The guard, Rollmeyer, hand on his holstered gun butt, hit her with the beam of his flashlight, then smiled when he recognized who she was. Part of his job was forestalling interruptions, so he walked over to her without calling out.

Lise hadn't been sure about what would happen when she got to this point. She couldn't have known ahead who the guard would be or how he would react to her, or how much he might know. She had gone over several possibilities, and decided to let the guard lead the way into this wilderness.

"Didn't know you was here, ma'am." Rollmeyer kept his voice low, standing close beside her on the soft sand. "They're going to be a while yet. You want me to take you around front, let you in that way?"

"The house is so hot. I'll wait out here until they're finished." She had her hand inside her bag, trading the automatic for something more appropriate to the situation. "Been a long time, Rollmeyer. Talk to me. How've you been?"

"Can't complain."

Hand in the bag, she wrapped her fingers around the wooden handle of the hotel ice pick. "Don't you have a hug for an old friend?"

Rollmeyer, who's job was following orders, and whose inclination was to cop any feel he could, seemed confused for just a moment. Then he opened his big arms and took a step toward her. She used the forward thrust of his body to help drive the ice pick up into his chest. Holding on to the handle, she could feel his heart beating around the slender blade, pump, pump, pump, before he realized something had happened to him. By then it was too late. She stepped back, withdrawing the blade, met his dumb gaze for another three count, watched the dark trickle spill from the tiny hole in his shirt, before he fell, face down. His eyes were still open, sugared with grains of white sand, when she left him.

Luther stayed close to her, his bulk providing a shield while she lay on her belly beside the pool and rinsed away Rollmeyer's blood from her glove and from the ice pick. With the dog, she ducked back into the shelter of the oleander hedge to watch the meeting proceed inside.

Creatures of habit, her husband and the Congressman were holding to schedule. By the time Lise arrived, they had eaten dinner in the elegant dining room and the housekeeper had cleared the table, leaving the two men alone with coffee and brandy. Genteel preliminaries over, she watched her husband go to the silver closet and bring out a large briefcase, which he set on the table. He opened the case, and smiling like Santa, turned it to show the contents to the Congressman, showed them to Lise also in the reflection in the mirror over the antique sideboard: money in bank wrappers, three-quarters of a million dollars of it, the going price for a crucial vote on the federal level — the vote in question of course having to do with permits for Vegas-style casinos on tribal land.

There was a toast with brandy snifters, handshakes, then goodbyes. Once business had been taken care of, she knew her husband would leave immediately and the Congressman would stay over for his special treat.

Lise dropped low behind the hedge when her husband, smiling still, crossed the patio and headed for the garage. She had the .380 in firing position in case he came looking for Rollmeyer. But he didn't. He went straight to the garage and started his Rolls.

As soon as he was out of sight, Lise moved quickly. Her husband would back down the drive to the road and signal the call girl who was waiting there in her own car, the call girl who always came as part of the Congressman's package. Lise knew she had to be finished within the time it would take for the whore to drive into the vacant slot in the garage, freshen her make-up, spray on new perfume, plump her cleavage, and walk up to the house.

With Luther lumbering at her side, Lise crept into the dining room through the patio door just as her husband's lights cleared the corner of the house. The Congressman had already closed his case of booty and set it on the floor, and was just finishing his brandy when she stepped onto the deep carpet.

"Lise, dear," he said, surprised but not displeased to see her. He rose and held out his arms toward her. "I had not expected the pleasure of your company."

Lise said nothing as she walked up within a few feet of him. Her toe was touching the case full of money when she raised the .380, took aim the way her father had taught her, and fired a round into the Congressman's chest, followed it, as her father had taught her, with a shot into the center of his forehead.

Luther, startled by the noise, began to bark. The housekeeper in the kitchen made "ah ah" noises and dropped something onto the floor. Lise tucked the gun under the Congressman's chest, picked up the case of money, and left.

Behind the hedge again, Lise waited for the call girl to walk in and help the housekeeper make her discovery. The timing was good. Both women faced each other from their respective doorways, shocked pale, within seconds of the shooting.

Through the quiet, moonless night, Lise walked back to the hotel along the same sandy path. She stowed the case behind a planter near the pool and continued on a block to place a call.

Rollmeyer would be a complication, but the police could explain him any way they wanted to. Lise dialed 911.

"There's been a shooting," she said. She gave the address, identified the Congressman as the victim and her husband as the shooter. Then she went to another phone further down the street and made a similar call to the press and to the local TV station.

When she heard the first siren heading up the road to the house, she was mailing an unsigned note to the detective who had investigated her father's death five years ago, a note that explained exactly why her husband and the Congressman were meeting in the desert in the middle of the summer and what her husband's motives might be for murder — for two murders. And why the bullets taken from the

Congressman should be compared with the two taken from her father. And where the assets were hidden and the skeletons buried. Chapter and verse, a fitting eulogy for a man who would never again see much open sky, whose every movement would be monitored in a place where punishment came swiftly, where he would never, ever have a key to his own door or the right to make the game plans. Trapped, for the rest of his life.

When the note was out of her hand, she finally took off the surgical gloves. Lise raised her face to catch a breeze that was full of sweet, clean desert air, looked up at the extravagance of stars in the moonless sky, and yawned. It was over: agenda efficiently covered, meeting adjourned.

On her way back to the hotel Lise stopped at an all-night drug store and bought an ice cream bar with some of Henry LeBeau's money. She ate it as she walked.

The manager was standing in front of the hotel watching the police and paramedics speed past when Lise strolled up.

"Big fuss." Lise stood on the sidewalk with the manager and finished her ice cream. "You told me it was dead around here this time of year."

"It's dead, all right." The manager laughed her dry, lizard laugh. "Lot of old folks out here. Bet you one just keeled over."

Lise watched with her until the coroner's van passed them. Then she took the manager by the arm and walked inside with her.

Lise saw the light of excitement still dancing in the manager's dark eyes. Lise herself was too keyed up to think about sleep. So she said, "I have another bottle of wine in my room. Let's say we have a little nightcap. Talk about crooks and the good old days."

GHOST CAPER

Rollie had to run through three backyards and under a dozen dark windows before he got his hard on. More effort than usual, and that worried him. But now the boner felt good, rubbing against the inside of his sweats with every step he took.

The night was ideal for capering. Rollie imagined how the crime report would read: At 0100 hours, the weather was dry and overcast, the temperature in the low sixties range. The crime scene area was residential with commercial activity along the major cross streets, Sunset Boulevard to the north and Santa Monica Boulevard to the south. A nice, clean report, he hoped. He would put in a request for a copy. The best part of it, he smiled to himself, would be the last line: No suspect description.

Rollie ducked down a short alley off Hampton and cut through the first yard he found that had no yapping dog. The yard was small and well-kept, behind a small, well-kept house. The only light came from a TV in a den at the back. In the flickering blue light he could see two shiny bodies undulating on the couch, layered one on top and one below.

Dense oleander bordered the redwood patio deck. He slipped into the shelter of its clipped branches to watch the lovers. His dark clothes made him feel invisible, powerful like a ghost on the couch between them. He stroked himself in the rhythm they set, breathing hard for them.

The night air was soft, fragrant with jasmine and clipped lawn. So nice, he could have finished himself right there. But he forced himself away, to stay focused, stay on task, because he knew *they* would be in the next block, or the next. Finishing without them would be a big-time disappointment.

He backed away from the cover of the oleander, his black sneakers as quiet as a shadow's steps on the damp grass. He went through a gate at the side of the house and, staying low, crossed the sloping front yard.

When he came out on Genesee, walking, Rollie saw the first police unit parked less than a block away, facing north toward Sunset. For a moment he savored the discovery. He had known they would not fail him, but now it was a sure thing. If they looked into their rear view mirror, they would see him, and, if the light hit just right, they would know him. He smiled wide for them as if they had asked him to say "cheese." With a sudden sadness at the transitory nature of this delight, he wished he could have a snapshot, a memento from a memorable evening.

Rollie was sorely tempted to tease at that point, do something closer near the edge of dangerous, to test them, see how much they had learned from him. Resisting the urge prolonged the pleasure. Already, he felt that if he so much as touched himself he would explode. But it was still too soon.

They never travelled alone. If there was one car out looking for him, he was certain there would be others. They could try to be unobtrusive, but he would easily spot their cars, generic American makes with dark paint jobs, oversized blackwalls, and a little antenna on the trunk. They might as well have sent black and white units after him.

It was mid-week and nothing else was happening in West Hollywood — he had checked the radio calls before setting out. There should have been enough units available to stake out the entire neighborhood, double the normal: West Hollywood straddled the jurisdiction between L.A.P.D. and the county sheriffs. If the call was heavy enough, they would both roll out. Rollie didn't worry about their number, only that they were good at their work.

The target he had picked was two blocks south, on Norton. Walking casually, he stooped at the end of a driveway to scoop up a throw-away advertiser. He slipped off its rubberband, awkward work with the clingy surgical gloves, and made a show of looking the paper over as he walked easily up the drive toward the lighted house. At the first sculpted shrub, he ducked out of view from the street.

He vaulted a low picket fence that separated this yard from the neighbor's, then skulked through the prickly shrubbery and climbed over another pair of fences, until there was only a vacant house with a room addition in process between him and his target house. Construction debris, bits of two-by-four, bent nails, twists of baling wire, made the going treacherous underfoot. Still, it was a good launching pad. There were no house lights, no inhabitants to rouse if he made a misstep.

He spotted a second car and knew the play was on. Taking cover behind an untrimmed hedge, and then a pile of new lumber, he made his way to the side of the dark vehicle.

Once again he felt the little electric trill in his groin as he rose to peer into the car window. He had his hand halfway to his waistband before he stopped himself. Instead, he reached into his pocket to finger the card he had tucked there, his ace in the hole, proof of membership in the club if things suddenly went wrong.

The car was empty. So, they were out on foot, hunters looking for him. That was good. He smiled, loving the ultimate challenge to date: They had parked directly across the street from his target house.

Using their car as his cover this time, he stopped to listen. He heard the ordinary sounds of night birds, TVs, households after bedtime. No police radio static, no cop talk. Satisfied no one had spotted him, he crossed the street standing up.

He had chosen his target with care, watched it, scoped the neighborhood for a week, explored every possible route between target and home base. A good challenge, plenty of variables.

Other than location, the target was just ordinary, a duplex he figured rented in the fourteen-hundred a month range. By the standards of West Hollywood it was modest, but not impoverished, rent well within the grasp of a young executive laboring in the corporate proving ground. No big deal, no hotshot security system.

The front unit of the duplex was heavily landscaped with politically-correct, drought-resistent foliage that would help to conceal his movements. Assholes, he laughed under his breath, as he slipped silently through the shrubbery toward the rear unit. Dues paying, card carrying assholes.

He saw no sign of *them*. They could be hiding in any of the houses in the neighborhood, even behind the dusty junipers lining the driveway he was walking down. But they weren't. He knew them so well — he was them — he would have felt them.

Even if he were sure they weren't around, he would have been as cautious. Heightened awareness was an essential factor in good capering.

He approached the rear unit and tried the front door. Why overlook the obvious? The door was locked, as were the windows on either side. He walked around to the small back patio and tried the sliding glass door. It was locked, but the slider was loose in its track, a cheap aluminum frame. Grasping the top edge of the slider, he slowly, carefully lifted it. At first, the door resisted, but the latch popped free of the jamb and the whole side came out of the track without so much as a squeak. He moved it aside just enough to slip inside.

The first thing he did was walk through the dark apartment and unlock the front door, in case he had to leave in a hurry. Then he went back and replaced the slider into its track and locked it. In the morning, while the investigating officers and deputies wrote their reports, the tenants would beat themselves up about forgetting to lock the front door.

Preliminaries taken care of, Rollie was free to roam.

The apartment was smaller than he had expected. Two bedrooms, living room, dining alcove, kitchen, a single bath. The furnishings were relatively spare, more taste than cash evident in their selection. The VCR was new, the TV was at least six-years old. There was a decent CD-tape player combination in an expensive glass-fronted cabinet — the nicest piece in the room.

He walked down the short, carpeted hallway that led to the bedrooms, being quiet, but not so quiet that he eliminated all the possibilities.

The first bedroom seemed to function as a study or small office. Accustomed to the dark, he picked out a PC, a FAX and a modem hookup on a desk that was no more than a hollow-core door laid over two sawhorses. Opposite this desk, there was a Stairmaster exerciser like the one in his den at home. Works hard, stays fit, he thought, with this added insight judging again the path of escape and his own speed.

With the apartment's layout committed to memory, Rollie went back out to the short hall. The bedroom door opposite was slightly ajar. Taking his time, moving like a ghost, he pushed it open.

In the soft yellow glow of a small night light, he saw two nude figures in the queen-size bed. He looked at them closely. This was West Hollywood; if they were both men, he would leave. But he saw painted toenails sticking out of the tangle of sheets, a spill of long hair across one of the pillows, and, below, a dark triangle with nothing protruding between the legs.

The single blanket had fallen to the floor, atop a pair of slacks. Rollie picked up the slacks and rifled the pockets. The fabric was nice, a step above Penney's, a step above this neighborhood. In the left front pocket he found a money clip with about a hundred dollars. He slipped it into his own pocket with his emergency Pass-Go card.

There was a matching suit coat draped over a bentwood chair, but its pockets held nothing more interesting than a tiny vial of coke and a narrow tie clasp. Nothing that couldn't easily be replaced, so he left it intact.

He picked up the watch on the nightstand, an older model Rolex with a crack in the crystal, changed the time and the date, and put it back. Never take anything with a serial number was rule one. The bedside alarm clock was set for five A.M. He shut it off.

This was a man's bedroom. A single man's, with no women's clothing in the deep closet. He picked up the woman's high-heeled shoes from the floor beside the bed and stuffed them inside his sweatshirt.

The woman stirred in her sleep, tossing off the sheet to expose her firm, surprisingly large young breasts. He went over to the bed and ran one finger along his erection, the other along her slender calf. She sighed softly and rolled against her bed partner, nestling her face into his hairless chest. Her partner drew her close and sleepily stroked her buttocks. As her lips began to move against his small, dark nipples, the intruder traced the graceful curve of her neck. Just to do it.

As the sounds in the bedroom grew heavier, he slipped into the bathroom. It was a little messy, the counter cluttered with the sort of hair junk and sprays he expected from what he had learned about the occupant. On the glass shelf under the mirror he found an old-fashioned shaving mug and a straight razor, like he'd seen in old movies. He picked up the razor and opened it, ran his finger lightly along the fine blade. So sharp it sliced through the his thin latex glove.

At least, he thought, here was a yuppie toy that was worth something. He closed the razor and put it back on the shelf next to the soap mug.

He left the bathroom and walked through the bedroom and out into the hall. The couple in the bed had settled back to sleep. The woman had rolled away from her partner, who was facing the far wall, snoring lightly.

He gave the house one more going over. In the kitchen, he found a candle, placed it in a cereal bowl, and lit it. He figured it would take a few hours to burn down. When the occupant and his guest came up for air again, and found they had overslept, the candle would give them one more thing to worry about.

His second pass through the small office turned up a nice gold overlay pen and pencil set. He could use them for writing burglary reports, so he slid the set into his pocket. There was nothing else he could think of to do.

He went to the front door, opened it, then paused, looking out toward the street, feeling unusually unfulfilled. No one was waiting for him. The pressure against the inside of his sweats had collapsed.

The entire caper had been nothing. He felt disappointed, depressed. Deprived of his due.

In the very beginning, merely thinking about capering had done it for him. Now every nocturnal outing demanded more of him: more danger, more challenges, more close calls. Push yourself to the limits, he always told them. But for himself, the limits kept moving away from him, always just beyond his grasp.

When he turned on his heel and walked back inside, headed straight for the bathroom, he was fueled with anger. There were hot tears in his eyes the second time he entered the bedroom, this time with the folded razor in his left hand.

The woman breathed softly, embracing her pillow. Rollie leaned over her and kissed her lightly on the ear. Still asleep, she turned toward him. He put his lips over hers, drew in her warm, sleepy breath. As her mouth opened to receive him, he opened the razor and drew the blade across her throat.

He kissed her hard now, pressed her shoulders against the bed, held her still as she struggled against death. The throes lasted only seconds, made no more noise than the sighs she had made in her sleep.

When she was gone, Rollie moved his mouth down over her erect nipple, tasted the warm, salty blood that flowed from the wound.

The power of what he had done almost overwhelmed him. He felt a surge, like the rush of the sea filling his head, threatening to sweep him under. For support, he backed against the wall and took a deep breath, her scent still on his face, the taste of her on his tongue.

In the dark, the blood streaming from her neck looked like a long, sinewy black ribbon that trailed across her shoulder, coursed down her slender white arm. She was beautiful. He loved her.

With his gloved fingers, he lifted her arm, placed it gently over the man's back. Desperately, Rollie wished he could be there to watch the man discover that, right there in the bed next to him, his lover had been unfaithful. Unfaithful with a ghost.

For a moment, he felt a pang knowing he, too, had been unfaithful. Of all the transgressions Valerie had accused him of, adultery had never been among them. The secret knowledge of his conquest thought cleared his head, cheered him to continue.

Planning was the key, and he was way off schedule, had spent far too much time inside. Meticulous even in his hurry, Rollie picked up a dirty white gym sock from the floor beside the bed, pulled it over his hand and carefully, lovingly, wiped the razor clean before he returned it to the bathroom shelf.

The front door was ajar as he had left it. Still with the sock on his hand, he went out, locking the door behind him.

Concealed again by the junipers at the edge of the front yard, he stopped to view the stakeout car across the street, saw that it was still unoccupied.

He knelt down and dug a small hole in the freshly turned garden, then buried the sock and the inverted gloves. Sometime in the future someone might find it all, but crusted with dirt, rotted from the sprinkler water, none of it would be of value to the hunters.

Where were the hunters, Rollie wanted to know, feeling distressed that they had fallen down on him after all of his efforts. He knew that when police reached the point in their careers where they were put on plain-wrap stakeout they definitely did not like to be out on foot. They liked to be in their cars, warm and comfy. He knew from his own experience that the cardinal rules for experienced police were never go hungry, never get wet, never get cold, and never breathe hard. That's what they had rookies for. Didn't these guys know that? Hadn't he taught them anything?

He looked down the street both ways, but still saw no sign of anyone. He reached inside his sweatshirt and he took the woman's shoes, arranged them carefully on the hood of the police car. Shoes of a lover met and lost in the course of an evening; he wanted to keep them.

Once they saw his trademark on the car, every black and white unit in the area would deploy, not to mention helicopters, and, if they got excited enough, L.A.P.D. units circling the outside perimeter. Looking for the ghost.

Feeling a little better, thinking about the reaction of the stakeout team when they got back into the car, he headed for home. After the first rush, though, thinking didn't do it for him any more. He felt robbed.

"Hey you! Halt."

He spun toward the voice, saw the uniformed figure and the mobile police radio in his hand. He knew he had virtually no time before the deployment began — cops, dogs, and that fucking helicopter. Police cars were certainly rolling in to seal off the area. He knew they expected him to behave like any other burglar. Run, and try to find a place to hide. Then they would bring in the dogs and sniff him out. And, if he were like the others, that would be the end of him.

What made it fun, he grinned, was that he wasn't like the others.

He sprinted between the houses, vaulted the first cinderblock wall in his path, and kept running. He reached Lexington and glanced back toward Genesee, saw the first black and white pull up to the intersection. They had been fast, so maybe they were good, too. With all his heart, he hoped so.

He crossed Lexington in mid-block at a dead run. As he reached the far curb, he heard the car bearing down behind him. He knew he had breached the first line of containment, but the good part was, there was more to come.

The first helicopter came whooping in the sky, maybe thirty-five or forty seconds away from where he was. But in thirty-five or forty seconds, he could be a long way into somewhere else.

In his black shoes, Rollie ran down a driveway, through an open gate and into a back yard that blessedly had no loose dog. Like all yards in the area, it was small and separated from its neighbors by an easily scaleable fence. His mind was clear, his movements sure. This chase is what it had all been about. The fresh boner slamming against the inside of his sweats was the proof.

As he hit the grass on the far side of the fence, he disturbed the dreams of a German shepherd sprawled, chained, next to a redwood doghouse. The dog got up and barked at him, but made no attempt to chase him. Rollie slowed to taunt the dog just a little. But the dog saved his energy for old ladies and paper boys.

A wooden gate blocked the driveway. He hardly broke stride as he rolled over it. The gate wasn't latched so it moved with him. He rode it into the front yard, waved at the shepherd as a farewell, then bounded across Hampton.

He ran full out between houses, expecting the helicopter to pick him out at any moment. He made it to Fountain Avenue, and took a big chance: he ran along the sidewalk, in the open, to Curson. He could hear the helicopter overhead, feel the disturbance in the air, see the trees move, making shadow monsters in the night. But the light hadn't yet found him so he continued to run in darkness.

All around, he heard the approaching cars as the police tried to seal him inside their snare. He had only a little further to go. The best for last.

When he turned north on Curson, he was sweating, but he wasn't winded. All the training in the hills of Elysian Park above the police academy was paying off. He would have energy to spare when the payoff came.

He heard a car brake close behind him, heard the two sets of footsteps and the shouting. He risked a glance, felt relieved when he saw they were no one he knew. At this point, the card in his pocket had lost its magic to save him, had become instead a ticket to the wrong side of the barbed wire.

Both officers were in full stride behind him, little wiry guys in good shape. If he had been the pursuer, he would have relied on the car for as long as possible. Maybe, he thought, the officers liked it better this way, the excitement of the chase canceling out the obvious and efficient. He could relate to it, but not condone it.

At Delongpre Avenue, he turned right. He knew he could outrun almost any cop, but he couldn't outrun their radios or their helicopter.

With only a couple of short blocks to go, the chase was more a matter of timing than strategy. He sprinted across Sierra Bonita and found himself in the vortex of approaching red lights. The helicopter spot played all around him, making the shadow monsters dance with him.

The street was a cul-de-sac that dead-ended in front of a library. He knew, because he had done his research, that neighborhood kids had cut shortcut holes through the chain link fence around the library. He found his hole and was through it without missing a step. Across a slippery wet lawn, another parking lot, then one last fence with the same ease. He came out on Gardner and saw his goal two houses further down the block.

At the moment the helicopter finally passed directly overhead he was sheltered by a huge old pepper tree. His movement was lost among the shadows of the wildly blowing branches as the chopper moved on.

An L.A.P.D. cruiser careened off Sunset and roared down Gardner, headed straight at him. He grinned, risking a quick touch to his full-on erection: they were too late.

He rolled under an oleander hedge and emerged in his own sideyard. Without straightening all the way up, he reached the door, turned the knob and was embraced by the warm after-dinner aroma of his kitchen.

Overhead, he heard the circling helicopter, saw the revolving shadows it cast as it passed over the street. They had come close this time, beautifully close.

The sounds of the search continued outside in the night around his well-kept bungalow as he hurried down the hall, struggling to get out of his shirt, dropping it to the carpet as he ran. He was in pain; the pressure in his testicles was almost more than he could tolerate.

Valerie was asleep, curled up on her side of the king-size bed. He stumbled out of his sweatpants, spilling from the pocket the stolen money clip, the gold pen and pencil, his own police photo I.D. card.

Before Valerie could waken and protest, he stripped the covers away from her and rolled her on her back. He knelt over her, put his mouth over her small silk-covered breast, groped under the slippery gown fabric to find her warm pubis.

She opened her eyes and pushed her hard little fists against his chest.

"You've been running again," she said. "You stink. Be a sport this time and go take a shower first."

"Can't wait," he moaned, spreading her legs apart as he lowered himself down on her. He thrust himself deep inside her, ignoring the sharp intake of her breath, her nails digging into his shoulders. Three long, shuddery strokes, and the caper was over.

Once again, the ghost had won.

BE YOUR OWN BEST FRIEND
by Alyson Hornsby and Wendy Hornsby

Red, gooey, disgusting Sloppy Joe filling oozed out of Carey's sandwich and glopped into her lap before she could catch it with her napkin. A grimace formed on her already gloomy face. Several kids sitting near her at the lunch benches looked over and giggled, others cupped their hands to a friend's ear and whispered something that produced laughter. Carey raised her chin and looked at them, and tried to smile as if she weren't embarrassed while she dabbed at the spreading mess on her lap.

Carey wished that her mom hadn't given her such a messy lunch. Ever since Mom was transferred to Findlay Creek, lunch was usually dinner leftovers, even if dinner had been take-out.

Feeling as red in the face as the stain on her jeans, Carey gathered the remains of her lunch and carried it over to the trash cans, getting a second, smaller, red glob on her clothes in the process. As she walked past the other kids, she wished for at least one of them to call her over to talk, or to just say something, anything, to her. She tried to smile and make eye contact, but already everyone seemed to have forgotten she was ever there. The other eighth graders at the lunch benches just continued to chat with their own little groups, looking cozy and content. In every new school, it was always the same for Carey.

Findlay Creek Middle School was Carey's sixth new school in the two years since her parent's divorce. Being the new kid all the time was difficult, especially for someone as shy as Carey. She tried her best to meet people, trying to look like someone who could be a friend, hoping anyone would respond to her. Every time she finally broke through the barrier of silence and met someone she could talk with at school, Mom would be assigned to a new project at work, they would move, and Carey would have to start all over.

"You'll make new friends," Mom always said. How do you make *new* friends when you never had old friends? Carey wanted to know. There had been a time, in Kansas, when she saved herself from being devoured whole by the monster of loneliness by making up a friend to talk to. Talking to herself made everyone, especially her mother, think she was nuts.

Carey wiped her hands and sat back down on the end of the bench with her knees tucked up to her chest to hide the stain on her jeans. She peered off through the fence beyond the basketball court and tried to appear fascinated with the brown grass and withering flowers on the far side. If she had to be alone, at least she wanted to appear as if she was alone on purpose. Her one consolation was that Monday was half over. Only four more lunch periods to endure that week.

That evening, Carey was at home in her room, finishing her homework, when her mother came home. Mrs. Parker rushed into her daughter's room and, before Carey could say anything, went into a long speech about the details of her hectic day. She paused only long enough to plant a light kiss on Carey's forehead. Carey sat patiently, as she always did, waiting for Mom to finish. After at least ten minutes, the usual question came.

"How was your day, dear?"

"Same as everyday," Carey said, shrugging her shoulders.

"Meet anyone interesting?" Mrs. Parker slipped off her high heels and sat on the bed beside Carey. She combed her fingers through her daughter's curly hair as if trying to bring some order to the unruly mass. "I hope you're making an effort. I don't want a repeat of what happened in Kansas. Remember what Dr. Osgood told you, 'You have to be a friend to have a friend.' "

"I try, Mom. But everyone is in a group, and they don't want me around. Small towns are the worst. Everyone has been friends since kindergarten. They look at me as if I'm an alien."

"Nonsense. It's all in your attitude. I moved around a lot as a kid. It isn't so difficult if you put some effort into it."

"But you're outgoing, and I'm not. I'm too weird, Mom. Nobody wants me around."

"You're certainly silly." Mrs. Parker showed her impatience with her daughter. "Analyze the problem, then find a solution. What do you want, Carey?"

"What do I want?" Carey faced her mother squarely. "I want to go home. I want Dad and Grandma and all my friends living on our same street again, the way it used to be. I want someone to know who I am."

"Then go out and introduce yourself to someone." Mrs. Parker picked up her shoes. "Dinner in twenty minutes."

When her mother was safely out of earshot, slipping something into the microwave no doubt, Carey dared to mimic her mom quoting Dr. Osgood, the nerdy psychiatrist in Kansas: "Be your own best friend. You're only as lonely as you want to be." Dr. Osgood had spouted the same dopey clichés to her every day of the two weeks she was stuck in his clinic. "When the world hands you lemons, make lemonade."

The microwave dinged. Dinner was ready.

Tuesday morning, Carey walked to school reciting Dr. Osgood's clichés to herself. At first, she only ran them over in her mind, but pretty soon, she was saying them out loud, imitating the fat-nosed doctor. Then she started answering him back. She didn't realize how loud she was speaking until, two blocks from school, the red-headed girl, Brooke, who sat in front of her during Spanish class, turned around and gave her a look as if, truly, Carey was completely nuts.

"Who are you talking to?" Brooke asked.

"Myself," Carey answered.

Brooke waited for her to catch up. "What are you talking about, then?"

"Reciting my Spanish, *Donde esta el sanitario?*" Carey said, too embarrassed to tell her the truth.

"*El sanitario es ...*" was as far as Brooke got before she started to laugh. "I always think that means the boys bathroom. Shouldn't the girls bathroom be *la sanitaria?*"

Carey felt herself blush, but for once she didn't duck her head and drop back. Instead, she laughed right along with Brooke. It felt so good to walk with someone across campus that she almost couldn't stop laughing after the bell rang. For the first time in a very long time, Carey had someone to eat lunch with.

After school, Carey rushed to find Brooke.

"*La sanitaria es en mi casa,*" Brooke said, tugging Carey's backpack. "And that's where I'm going. My house, that is. Want to come? You live on the same block as me. I watched you move in. Your mom works with my dad. Actually, your mom took over my dad's old job. My dad was assigned to a new project."

"Every time my mom gets a new project," Carey said, "we move."

"Same with us. We're leaving in a week. Albuquerque, New Mexico, this time."

Carey suddenly felt like crying, and she could see that Brooke was unhappy, too. They had just met, and now Carey was going to lose her only friend.

For the next week, Carey and Brooke were almost inseparable. Finally, Carey had someone who knew about her life. Really knew about her. Carey's mother and Brooke's father had been playing a sort of leap-frog with each other, moving into and out of many of the same towns according to the wishes of their employer. Carey and Brooke found that they had attended several of the same schools and lived in the same neighborhoods, had been chased by the same big, mangy dog in Tulsa, Oklahoma. Even if they had never lived in the same place at the same time, they'd had so many similar experiences that they began to feel as if they had known each other for a very long time.

Carey and Brooke avoided talking about Brooke's upcoming move until the afternoon of the last day. Brooke had treated them both to an ice cream cone. They were sitting atop a picnic table in the park, finishing their cones, when Brooke said, "I always hate moving."

"Then don't go." Carey felt close to tears. "Stay here with me."

"I did that once. I ran away and hid because I didn't want to move until the end of the school term."

"What happened?" Carey asked.

"My parents found me."

Carey had an idea that made her heart pound in her chest. "You could stay with me and my mom until the term is over. Ask your parents."

"And you could spend the summer with me," Brooke said, sounding as excited as Carey felt.

Carey grabbed Brooke by the hand and almost dragged her from the table. "There's no time to waste. Let's go call them."

When she came home from work at seven, Carey's mother skipped the usual retelling of her day. Instead, she put her arm around her daughter. "I know you'll miss Brooke, Carey. But imagine how much her parents would miss her if she stayed here with us. All is not lost, though. Her parents and I have decided that we'll send the two of you to the same camp this summer."

"This summer?" Carey's throat seemed to close up, choking back the words she wanted to say.

"Summer is only a few months away."

Carey knew that summer was exactly fifty-two lunch periods away.

Mom slipped out of her heels. "You've made one friend already. You can make another." Then she walked off toward the kitchen, leaving Carey to fight back her tears alone.

The next morning, moving day, dawned cold and gray. Carey thought that the weather suited the occasion perfectly. Feeling sad, Carey walked over to Brooke's house.

Brooke met her with a big hug. "Don't forget me, Carey."

"Don't go," Carey begged, and then felt ashamed when Brooke started to cry.

Brooke's mother came over and said it was time to leave. "Brooke will write to you as soon as we get to Albuquerque. Summer will be here sooner than you think."

Then Brooke was gone.

That night, it rained. Not a little rain, but a huge storm with thunder and lightning and water pouring down in a relentless torrent. Carey's mother called from downtown. "It's raining so hard, it isn't safe for me to drive. I'll be home as soon as I can get there. Make yourself some dinner, and don't wait up for me." Carey didn't feel like eating.

Carey sat beside her living room window, watching the rain. She worried about Brooke's family driving through the storm. And she worried about going to school the next day, all alone again.

The night was so dark that the window mirrored the lighted room behind her. Carey leaned her forehead against the cold pane and looked into the reflection of her eyes on the glass, and pretended they were Brooke's. "Come back," she said, and then waited for Brooke to respond.

Now and then, a gust of wind would snap a tree branch against the side of the house with a pop that sounded like someone knocking on a door. Every time it happened, Carey imagined herself opening the door and finding Brooke standing there. And then she imagined what they would say to each other.

"How was the trip to Albuquerque?" Carey would ask.

"We couldn't get through," Brooke would say. "The roads were flooded."

Brooke would be wet and shivering, and Carey would bring her inside. "Come in and get warm, tell me all about it."

Thinking about her friend, pretending to have a long conversation with her, made Carey feel better. She was glad her mother was elsewhere, because she knew what would happen if Mom came in and found her talking to someone who wasn't really there.

"What do you think, Dr. Osgood?" Carey imitated her mother's voice of concern. "The girl is talking to herself again. What shall we do with her?"

"You're only as lonely as you want to be," she answered, mocking old Dr. Osgood by speaking so deeply it tickled her throat. "Be your own best friend."

Rain beat steadily on the roof, sounding like a constant drum roll. The room had grown cold. Carey pushed away from the window and went over and curled up on the sofa under a quilt her grandmother had made. She didn't realize she had fallen asleep until she heard a knock at the door. At first she was certain that it was the wind and the tree again. After the third sharp rap, she decided otherwise.

Untangling herself from the quilt, Carey went over and opened the door.

Brooke, standing under the porch light, her drenched clothes clinging to her shivering frame, gave a little laugh and smiled at Carey.

Carey reached out to touch her friend because she was afraid that she was still asleep, and that Brooke was no more than a vision in her dreams. But Brooke's arm was wet and cold and as firm and real as

Carey's own. As she drew her into the living room, Carey asked Brooke, "How was the trip to Albuquerque?"

"We couldn't get through. The roads were flooded."

Carey took Brooke's wet coat and handed her the quilt that was still warm from her nap. "Where are your parents?" Carey asked.

"They're going to a hotel. They said I can stay here, if it's okay with your mom."

There was no mom around to ask, so of course it was all right. Carey heated them a can of soup while Brooke changed into dry clothes; one of Carey's flannel nightgowns, the one her father had sent last Christmas. After they ate, they locked the doors, turned out the lights, and climbed under the covers of Carey's twin beds. They talked through most of the night, half because they were waiting for Carey's mom, and the rest because there was so much to talk about. Sometime before dawn, they both drifted off to sleep.

By morning, the heavy rain had dwindled to a soft drizzle. When the alarm clock rang, Carey wakened, exhausted. Without disturbing Brooke, Carey got up and dressed for school. There was no reason for Brooke to get out of her warm bed that cold morning as she was no longer registered at Findlay Creek Middle School. Carey wished she could stay home, too.

As she walked toward her mother's room, Carey started making up aches and pains and various excuses why she should be excused from school. But her mother wasn't in her room. The only signs that her mother had made it home the night before were the pair of high heels left in the middle of the kitchen floor, and a note propped against the toaster.

"Sorry I had to leave before you got up this morning," the note said. "Glad everything is fine. See you tonight. Love, Mom."

Carey called her mother at the office. "I have a terrible cold," she said, talking through her nose and coughing twice. She didn't mention that Brooke was there, because then Mom would know Carey's cold was only an excuse to stay home.

Promising to call if she needed anything, Carey changed back into her nightgown and climbed back into bed. It was nearly noon when the two girls finally decided they needed food. They made a pile of cinnamon toast and spent the day in their night clothes, watching soap operas — which they found hysterically funny — and old movies on video.

Carey's mother called three times, and every time Carey neglected to mention Brooke. Brooke's parents never called at all. Somewhere around dusk, with rain falling hard once again, Carey's mother called a fourth time.

"I hate to do this to you, honey, especially since you've been cooped up all day with that cold, but I have to work late tonight," Mom said. "I'll be home by bed time, I promise."

Carey and Brooke went to bed early, and never saw Mom. On the second day, Carey pretended to dress for school, but after Mom left for work, she stayed home again. As she did on the third day, and the fourth, until a full week of school had slipped by without Carey ever facing the silent treatment at the lunch benches. Without any question, it was the best week Carey had spent during the entire last two years. She was never once, even for a minute, lonely.

Brooke's parents never called. Every evening, when Carey's mother arrived home, Brooke was already either asleep or in Carey's room reading by herself or out visiting her former neighbors. No one ever bothered to mention to Mrs. Parker that there was a house guest, and, except for mentioning how big Carey's appetite was all of sudden, Mrs. Parker never noticed. Not even on the weekend.

Once, on Sunday afternoon, Mrs. Parker almost walked right into Brooke with the laundry basket. "Put your things away," was all she said, handing Brooke the basket. Carey had watched the close encounter, and could hardly keep from laughing right out loud until she had Brooke safely inside her room with the door closed.

"When are we going to tell Mom you're here?" Carey asked.

"When my parents call," Brooke answered.

On the second Monday, the attendance office at Carey's school called, wanting to know where she had been all the previous week. At first, she was nervous about the trouble she would certainly get into. Then Brooke told her what to say.

"I have pneumonia," Carey said. "I just got out of the hospital. I don't know when I'll be back in school."

At noon, the two girls were sprawled on the living room floor in their nightgowns, going through old photo albums, laughing over Carey's pictures of her father and grandmother, and all the friends who had lived down the block. The girls were so involved with the pictures that they didn't hear Carey's mother come in.

"Carey?" Mrs. Parker was as pale as if she had seen a ghost, and that ghost was Carey herself. "What are you doing home?"

Carey shut the album in front of her. "Nothing."

"Your school called. They said you have been absent for six days."

Carey counted. "Only five and a half days." She turned toward Brooke for confirmation, but Brooke must have seen Mom and had managed to slip away in time.

"Who were you talking to?"

"Myself. Like Dr. Osgood said, Be your own best friend." She tried to laugh as if the phrase were an old familiar joke, but the look on her mom's face froze her.

Mrs. Parker placed her hand over Carey's forehead. "I'll call a doctor."

"I'm not sick."

Mrs. Parker took a deep breath as if trying to calm herself. She looked more worried than angry, and that made Carey feel terribly guilty.

"If you're not sick," Mrs. Parker said, "then why aren't you at school?"

Avoiding telling her mom something was different from coming straight out with a lie. Carey blurted the truth. "I stayed home because Brooke is here. She's been here since last Sunday night."

Carey expected a flood of questions, like where is she, and how did she get here, and why didn't you tell me? Instead, her mother stood absolutely still and silent for an entire minute, watching Carey the whole time. Mrs. Parker was so pale that Carey began to feel frightened.

"I'll get Brooke," Carey said, heading for her room. "She can tell you about it."

Brooke wasn't in the bedroom. Brooke wasn't anywhere. Carey rushed into the living room, where her mother was dialing the telephone.

"Maybe she went down to the park," Carey said. "I'll go get her."

Mrs. Parker stopped her. "I picked up the mail, Carey. There's a card for you. It was postmarked two days ago." She handed Carey a postcard with a desert scene on the front. Holding the telephone receiver to her ear, Mrs. Parker watched her daughter study the card.

"New Mexico, Land of Enchantment" was printed across the desert scene. Carey turned the card over and began to read. "Dear, Carey, *La sanitaria es en mi casa* in Albuquerque now."

"Dr. Osgood?" Mrs. Parker said into the telephone.

"My new house is nice, but I really miss you," Carey read. "I started school Thursday. Yuck!"

"Dr. Osgood, it's happened again. Shall I bring her to you?"

"See you next summer. Love, Brooke."

OUT OF TIME
by Alyson Hornsby and Wendy Hornsby

"Mom, did Nana have a lover?" My twenty-one-year-old daughter, Lainey, sat cross-legged on the floor of my mother's attic, an ancient steamer trunk open in front of her, an old shoebox full of snapshots resting across her knees. "This guy, whoever he is, is really good-looking."

"Nana, a lover?" I said. "Never."

"He is definitely a prince, Mom. And he's all over Nana. Look at him."

"Not now. My hands are full." I pulled a broken lamp from a jumble of dusty cast-offs in a far corner and sent it down the trash chute we had rigged from the attic window to a dumpster in the yard below.

Six months after my mother's funeral, we had finally managed to sell her old house, the house where I grew up. I had put off the task of attic and cellar cleaning, and all the memories stored there, until there was no more time to stall.

All weekend we'd had plenty of help. My brother and his wife and various old friends had all joined Lainey and me in a happy sort of campout, the accommodations becoming more and more Spartan as the furniture and rugs were disposed of, one room at a time. By Sunday night, most of the heavy work was finished, the general patching and repairing had been done, and there was new paint throughout.

Monday morning Lainey and I were alone in the house, and there was still more work to do than I thought it was possible to finish in the few days left to us. By the afternoon we were exhausted, over-whelmed, dirty and short-tempered as we felt the press of time. Just the same, that Monday was a rare pleasure: a full day alone together was a rarity since Lainey had moved away to college three years earlier.

Trying not to sound like a shrew, I said, "Honey, if you stop to look at every old picture, we'll never get the house ready for the new owners by Thursday."

"I know, I know." With the shoebox in her arms, she uncoiled from the floor and came over to me. Holding the picture that had captivated her so that I could see it, she said, "Just look at him, Mom. Do you know who he is?"

Dust motes swirled around us, an effect like a gauze filter before my eyes, as I looked at the face.

Four days spent sorting heirlooms and keepsakes and just plain junk Mother hadn't gotten around to tossing out had left me emotionally purged. Old issues that were stirred up with the dust I dealt with in turn and put away. By day two, I could gather up Mom's forty-five-years accumulation of frilly Mother's Day cards and her collection of baby teeth and send them all down the trash chute without an instant's hesitation. By day three even her antique teacups stirred little interest. Suddenly, however, a face gazing out of a faded photograph opened a deep, dark emotional closet I had forgotten existed, and left me short of breath and light-headed.

"That's my father," I said. "Your grandfather, Richard."

"Whoa. My grandfather?" Lainey grinned, happy at the discovery. "Go Nana. I can't feature her in a big romance with a guy this gorgeous. Nana wasn't what you would call a beauty or a bundle of laughs."

"She was once."

Lainey grew thoughtful. She brushed her fingertips across her grandfather's face before she put the picture back into the box, which she cradled in the crook of her arm. "You never talk about your father. All that you've ever said is that he died."

"I was only six-years-old, honey. I don't remember very much about him."

She watched me until I felt uncomfortable. To get out from under her stare, I said, "Will you help me move the big table from the corner?"

She sighed, and shrugged elaborately. Tucking a stray strand of hair under her bandanna, she walked with me through the maze of boxes marked "Goodwill," or labeled with the names of various friends and relatives. Men from my mother's church were going to haul away the leftovers for us on Wednesday.

"Nice table." Lainey knelt to examine the heavily carved legs. "Can I have it?"

"Certainly, but where would you put it?"

"I'm thinking about getting an apartment for my senior year. I can use the table as a desk."

"This is the first I've heard about an apartment."

"What's to tell? I don't want to live in the dorm with freshman scrubs. Besides, an apartment is cheaper than the dorm."

"Will you have a roommate?" I asked.

"Yes. We found a great place one subway stop from campus. It's great. All I need now is a desk."

"So you're more than just *thinking* about an apartment."

"I was going to tell you." She gave me a wry grin. "I'm an adult. I don't need my mom to co-sign the lease."

"Of course you don't." I patted her bare arm when what I wanted was to cradle her in my lap. "If you want the table, tag it or it'll end up at Goodwill."

With her shirt tail, Lainey polished a corner of the table top until the old mahogany shone. Looking at her reflection, she said, "You have Nana's picture on the family room wall with everyone else. Why isn't your father there beside her?"

"I don't know." I felt uncomfortable, challenged. "I guess I thought it would make Nana feel sad to see him."

"Why would she be sad? Grandpa Joe's picture doesn't make Grandma sad. Hell, she even blows him a kiss when she walks by it. You didn't take down Daddy's picture when he moved out, and we all know that Daddy makes you more than a little unhappy."

"Even if I don't see him anymore, he's still your father, and Grandma's son." I grasped one end of the table. "Help me, please."

"So, what happened to your father?" She was persistent.

"I told you, he died. Will you grab an end here?"

Lainey set the shoebox atop the table carelessly enough so that it spilled, snapshots slid out, scuffing a path through the dust. Her voice sounded tight. "You're doing it again, Mom."

"Doing what?"

"Shutting me out. What is the big deal? I thought we had established that I'm an adult. I don't need to be protected from the truth. And I think I'm entitled."

I started to protest, to defend myself. Then I looked at her sweet face, a face so much like my father's around the handsome eyes, and remembered him saying to my mother, "If you're angry with me, I wish you would simply say so."

"I'm sorry." I put my arm around Lainey. "I don't mean to shut you out. After my father died, mentioning him in this house was the biggest taboo. I loved him, I missed him terribly. But there was no one to tell how I felt. It still makes me uncomfortable to talk about my father because it was a forbidden topic for so long."

"Why all the silence? I mean, people die all the time."

"Nana had standards, even for the way people were supposed to die."

"Nana isn't here, Mom." Lainey smiled. "It's okay. Let it out."

"I don't know very much about what happened."

"Tell me what you know."

I shrugged. "My father died in Butte, Montana, six-hundred miles from here. He was a mining engineer, working on a project. Mother, Nana, got a call late one night. The next morning she went away on the train, and came home a week or so later with my dad in a shiny black coffin. That's what I remember most clearly, that big shiny coffin."

"What did she tell you happened to him?"

"She didn't," I said. "The only person who said anything to me was Essie the housekeeper. All she said was, 'Your father passed, you poor little thing. What will your mother do?'"

"That's cold."

"Nana was overwhelmed," I said, feeling defensive of my mother, so recently gone. "I'm sure that Nana planned to talk it over with me and your Uncle Dickie when she could be more composed. But she never did. Her pain was very private, and I'm sure she thought she was protecting us. After a while, the silence was just habit."

"I look at these pictures," Lainey said, "and I don't know who most of the people are. Are they your father's relatives? My relatives? Where are they now?" Lainey collected the spilled pictures, squaring the corners before putting them back into the box. She looked askance at me. "Nana owed you more."

"I was only a little girl," I said, wishing Lainey, for once, would let an issue drop. "Nana wanted to protect me and Uncle Dickie. I never got the whole story, so what I remember is just fragments, flashes from the past that are like watching those faded old snapshots spill."

"What do you remember?"

I thought for a moment before answering. "I remember Nana taking her good black dress out of the dry cleaner bag and changing the shiny buttons to plain ones. I remember holding Nana's overnight bag at the station, and how heavy it was. My teacher brought over my school work so I could do it at home, but I wanted to go be with my friends. There was a heavy fog the whole time Nana was gone. And I had a pain so intense one night that Essie called the doctor in."

"What was wrong with you?"

"Heartache. Loneliness."

"You had Uncle Dickie."

"He was just a baby," I said. "What puzzled me most was that no one came calling. This town is so small and so boring, that the biggest things that ever happen are weddings, funerals, and fires in green hay. The whole town will show up for a broken leg. I kept expecting neighbors and friends, the ladies guild from the church, to be here clucking over the terrible thing that had happened.

"I thought Mrs. Caldwell would make us the same big coconut cake she took to the Proski family when Walter fell under the wheels of his tractor. There should have been tuna noodle casserole with potato chip topping, and Jell-O. Nothing ever happened without some kind of Jell-O showing up. But not for us that time."

"That's precious. Poor Mom." Lainey hugged me. "Not even Jell-O?"

"Nothing and no one."

"That's mean. You were just little kids."

"It's the way Nana wanted things. The gossip would have been brutal, but she put a stop to it right away. There was no funeral even."

"What did Nana do, throw the coffin off the back of the train?"

"Almost. Essie dressed up Uncle Dickie and me to meet Nana at the station. We went from there directly to the cemetery. Dr. Wilby, the minister, came with us, and Mr. Harper from the mortuary — he took the coffin in his hearse — but nobody else. Not even the director of the Sunday school came, and she was without question the best crier in the whole town."

Lainey chuckled. "Seems so strange."

"It was. I asked Essie whether things were done differently when someone died out of town, if maybe all of the fuss and coconut cake happened wherever the person had died."

"What did Essie say to that?"

"'Don't get your good shoes wet.'"

"But there was some kind of service, wasn't there?"

"Dr. Wilby said a prayer, and Dad went straight into the ground. When I started to protest — I couldn't remember my dad's face, I wanted the coffin opened the way my grandfather's had been, just to be sure Dad was in there — Essie said, 'You hush, girl. Don't upset your Momma.' "

"What did Nana say?"

"Not a word. I think she was doped just so she could get through it. As soon as we got back home, she took Dad's portrait off the mantle, stowed his clothes and books, his rack of pipes and his golf clubs, and any other evidence that he had ever lived in our house into that trunk where you found the pictures. And he was never again spoken of."

"Not even to Uncle Dickie?"

"No."

"Do you and Uncle Dickie talk about it now?"

"Never."

"Don't you think you should? He has kids himself. Doesn't he deserve to know something about his father? I mean, you remember some stuff, but he was younger."

"You don't understand, Lainey. There are other factors involved that complicate things," I said, trying to make it clear that she shouldn't inquire further.

"I never will know if you don't tell me." Lainey took hold of one end of the table and lifted. "So, what did your father do that was so terrible? Suicide?"

"No," I said, lifting my end of the table. "He was shot by an irate husband."

"O-oh." Her eyes grew round, her mouth dropped for an instant as all the pieces seemed to fall into place. We set the table down near the top of the stairs. "So when Daddy ..."

"Excuse me." I didn't want her to see me cry, so I turned and fled down the stairs and out of the attic. My head was flooded with dust, but also with thoughts that hadn't entered my mind in years because I had tried so hard to forget they were even there. Somehow, one of those tricks of the mind, the enforced silence around my father and the impenetrable secrets that enshrouded my almost-ex-husband became all mixed up together, grief and anger doubled.

Marriage is a private world. My mother owed me some explanation. She did not owe me the whole truth. How much more was Lainey entitled to know about her father and me?

I remembered my mother coming off the train looking tired and fragile: white faced, dry eyed, her good black dress so wrinkled she might have worn it the entire five days she was gone. She held us by the hand, but allowed no one close enough to hold her. I was afraid that if I cried she would collapse, and it would be all my fault.

I could taste the saltiness of the stream of tears that ran down my cheeks. I took the stairs two at a time so that Lainey wouldn't hear me cry. The door to my old bedroom flew open and I ran for the mattress that was the only remaining furniture in the room, curling myself into a little ball just as I had that day when I was six years old and I learned that my father was gone. I wept for him and I wept for my mother, and for all the promises unfulfilled.

"Mom, you okay?" Lainey's voice wakened me from an exhausted sleep.

I raised my head to see her sweet face looking at me with worry and a little fear. I glanced at my reflection in the window and saw why she would be concerned about me. She had probably never seen me with red puffy eyes and a swollen nose. All through the divorce, I did my best to hide the depth of my feelings from her. Just as my mother had done.

I looked pathetic, felt pathetic, and I didn't want to show my weakness to Lainey. My daughter was so strong, I was afraid that she would just pity me.

"You've been asleep for an hour," she said. "I thought you might want to get cleaned up."

"Cleaned up for what?" I said. "What time is it?"

The doorbell sounded.

Lainey glanced at her watch, seemed almost panicky. "Oh, my God."

"Honey," I said, "Would you get the door?"

"Would you? I am a mess." She pulled off the bandanna she had wrapped around her hair. "I'll be right behind you, but I need a minute."

I tried to pull myself together as I went down to the front door. I heard Lainey's sandals on the bathroom floor upstairs, and the scratchy sound of a hairbrush, water running in the basin. Needing more than a quick brushing and a face wash myself, I merely combed my fingers through my hair and stood up straighter. There was no one in town I needed to impress, but I was my mother's daughter: there were standards.

The front door had been left open for fresh air, so there was only a screen separating my disheveled self from the tall young man on the porch.

His was a face I hadn't seen before, but he smiled as if we should be friends. Was he the grown son of one of my old neighborhood playmates? I stepped closer to the door.

"Hello," he said in a voice that sounded vaguely familiar. "Are you Mrs. Murphy, Lainey's mother?" As I opened the screen, he stepped forward with his hand extended; nervous yet excited. "I'm Paul. We spoke on the phone yesterday."

"Yes, I remember. Lainey's friend from college." I took the offered hand. He was handsome, dark hair and lots of teeth. He wore khaki shorts and a rugby shirt, a pair of very old Nikes, and a fair share of confidence. I was curious about him, and maybe a little wary. I said, "Nice of you to drop by. Do you live in the area?"

Before he had a chance to respond, Lainey was next to me, smiling, her hair brushed smooth, a glow on her cheeks. The worried face she had worn upstairs had vanished. When she turned to Paul, her happy expression was a revelation to me. "Good, you two have met."

"Come in, Paul." I stood aside. "Lemonade?" I asked. Exactly what my mother would have said, I thought, feeling suddenly old. Should I have offered him a beer?

Lainey put her arm through his as if by habit and led him inside and down the long hall to Nana's kitchen. I followed a few steps behind, watching them. Paul was telling Lainey about his train ride from school and she was laughing as I had never seen her laugh. Her eyes were bright and she gave his every word her rapt attention.

As she reached for glasses from the cupboard, she said, "Mom's giving us the most wonderful old table that's been in Nana's attic for who knows how many lifetimes. It'll be perfect for the computer."

I refrained from repeating, "Us." Instead, I excused myself, went upstairs, brushed my hair, washed my face, changed into a clean shirt. I'm not sure they noticed that I was gone.

I had not been expecting a visitor, especially one of this sort, and I wasn't sure what I was supposed to do. Lainey had dated in high school, so I was used to meeting boyfriends who came and went with the seasons. But this one seemed different. She had never even mentioned him to me, yet they seemed to be serious enough to want to live together. I couldn't imagine why she wouldn't want me to know about her relationship with Paul. I never thought she was the kind of person who kept secrets.

I walked back to the kitchen, feeling like a snoop. Lainey was standing alone cutting apples and arranging them on a plate with cheese and crackers.

"Paul is in the bathroom washing up. The train ride up from school was long and uncomfortable, you know how that can be," Lainey said nonchalantly as she placed an apple slice in the middle of a pinwheel of cheese. "Travel makes you feel so grungy. Must be the train air."

"You met Paul at school?" I said, grabbing an apple and a knife to join her.

"Chemistry class. Too ordinary, I know. Chemistry. He was my lab partner. He's really smart. He's pre-med."

"How old is Paul?"

"Twenty-one, like me."

"And he doesn't want to live with freshman scrubs next year, either?" I was obviously digging for information, and she knew it.

Lainey turned to me and looked me straight in the eye. She smiled an embarrassed smile, knowing that I had caught on. "Mom, Paul and I are planning to live together next year."

"I got that message," I said. "Aren't you rushing things?"

"I wanted to tell you about Paul a long time ago, but I thought you would be overwhelmed with Nana, and then Dad and everything. I knew that if you met Paul you would see how great he is and wouldn't think it was a big deal."

"You don't give me enough credit, Lainey. I think I have a right to know," I said.

"Of course you do, Mom. I just thought that it would make you uncomfortable. Since the divorce you've been kinda negative and withdrawn. I didn't want to give you a chance to say no until you'd met him. I promise, Mom, he's not like my dad, or your dad. When you get to know him you'll see that he's really great."

"I'm sure he is. Moving in together is a big step. How long have you known him?"

"Long enough."

"Are you two talking about marriage?"

"I don't think I ever want to get married." She looked me directly in the eye. "We all know how that turns out."

"Oh, sweetheart." I felt stung as I put my arm around her. "I have to admit I'm relieved; I think it's way too early to be planning a wedding. But marriage can be wonderful. Your dad and I had many very happy years."

"Happiness doesn't last forever. I mean, it would be great if it did, but I don't want to go through the hell that you had to go through. I saw what breaking up did to you, and now I'm seeing what it did to Nana." She looked so serious and so matter-of-fact. "I love Paul, but I'm too sensible to think that it will always be like this between us."

"No, it won't be. What if it gets better?" My heart ached, realizing the impact my experiences had on her. "Maybe Nana and I look like disasters to you. But knowing what I know, I wouldn't have done anything differently. And remember, you aren't us."

"I know all that. But why risk it? I know that Paul is good and honest, but I'm sure you and Nana thought the same things in the beginning. And look what happened. I'm not going to set myself up for the fall."

"Oh honey ..." I didn't know what to tell her. My marriage ended like a bad soap opera, and tragedy could certainly be a word applied to Nana's situation. Still, I knew that wasn't the only way. "I don't know which clichés to give you. But it all comes to the same thing: be friends first. When things got bad, too often I did what Nana did. I froze everyone out, including your dad. I thought all our problems would just go away if I pretended nothing was happening. I wasn't a very good friend to your dad when times got tough."

"Mom, are you blaming yourself for Daddy's affair?"

"No. That was his decision. If nothing else, the break-up could have been less traumatic if we had all been able to sit down together. We should have included you more. Like Nana, I assumed you knew all that you needed to know and were old enough to understand. You always seemed so strong. You were my little trooper."

"I stayed strong because of you. I was afraid that if I broke down, you would, too."

"I'm sorry I put that burden on you, Lainey. Trust me, I know how heavy that load is."

Lainey was misty eyed and the apple slice in her hand shook slightly. I looked at her and realized that I couldn't read her face. In some ways, this young woman was a stranger to me as she grew into her independence.

I said, "I love you Lainey. And I always loved your father."

She raised her head, but her eyes slid past me as Paul appeared at the doorway.

"Can she cook?" he said, pulling a stool up to the kitchen counter.

"No. But I can open a deli package." Lainey seemed to have recovered in his presence. She wore a smile I had never seen her wear, and one that I hoped she never lost. She pushed the beautifully arranged plate in front of him. "Eat up. I'll bet it's better than anything you could get in the club car. At least it's prettier."

"Thank you. It's nice to have a fully stocked kitchen instead of the dining hall, huh?" He stacked a piece of cheese and an apple slice together and took a bite. Looking straight into her eyes, he said, "It's beautiful, thank you."

"Any time." Lainey shrugged. "I was just telling Mom about the apartment."

"Good." He swallowed a bit hard, but managed to keep the smile. "We found a really great place, Mrs. Murphy. It was a steal."

"Tell me about it."

He did, his smile growing: one bedroom, an okay bathroom, a tiny kitchen off the living room that would be their study. An easy walk to the campus. I couldn't see anything under that warm smile that would suggest heartache down the road. He looked so hopeful and good. And trustworthy. Had my efforts to shield Lainey from unpleasantness made it impossible for her to trust?

"I hope you'll come see us once we've gotten settled," he said. "If you don't mind sitting on the floor."

"Lainey," I said, "I've kept a pair of Nana's rockers and the dining room chairs. Would you like to have any of them?"

"I would." She hesitated. "But you want them."

"Better that things are used than to have them gathering dust in my garage."

She reached across the table and took Paul's hand. "Mom's giving us the best old table. You'll love it."

I decided that at the moment I was one person too many in the kitchen. I finished my lemonade and excused myself.

"I'm going to go back up to the attic," I said. "Any volunteer help will be appreciated. There's so much work to be done. We'll never get this place packed up by Thursday unless we skip sleeping for the next few nights."

"We'll be up to help you in a little while," Lainey called after me. "Don't worry, we'll get it finished in time."

The old wooden stairs creaked as I climbed back to the attic. Strangely, my head felt clearer in the cloudy attic than it had downstairs. I found an unexpected comfort in the jumble and mess. I reached for a trash bag, ready to attack a pile of old newspapers when I saw the old mahogany table standing alone.

I grabbed a tag, wrote, "Goes in U-haul," and tied it to a leg. The table was old, even when my mother had bought it to put in the entry of the house just a few years after my father died. She had said that she would put flowers on it and pictures of her children so anyone who came to the house would see how beautiful we were. She said it made her happy to see our smiling faces when she came in the door. I don't know when the table moved up to the attic. Maybe she got tired of dusting picture frames: first there were two weddings, then four babies — my one and Dickie's three — christenings, graduations, too many milestones for one table. Or, maybe, there were too many reminders.

I found a clean rag and began to polish the table. Some of the frames had left marks on the surface, and I thought about all those faces, my family, past, present. Nana had paired one of my baby pictures with one of Lainey's in a tandem silver frame. How alike we were, she would say, and how I loved to hear it. She always attributed our best features to her side of the family, never mentioned Dad.

I have my mother's strong nose and high forehead, but I also have my father's full mouth, a legacy that is even more apparent on Lainey's face. She has his eyes, and her own father's long legs and peaches and cream skin.

By the time I heard Lainey's light footsteps and Paul's heavy ones bounding up the stairs, the old table shone like the treasure it had once been.

"Wow, Mom. It looks fantastic." Lainey's face was bright with pleasure. "Paul, don't you think it will be perfect?"

"It is perfect." Paul seemed to share her excitement as he ran his hand over the surface. "This is real furniture. I was planning to make a table out of a door and two saw horses."

"There are two extension leaves somewhere around here," I said. "You can make it larger."

"Thanks, Mom." Lainey hugged me. Her happiness was contagious.

"Too bad you didn't mention the apartment before Uncle Dickie drove off with all the dressers," I said.

She leaned into Paul, wrapped her arm around him, and gave me a sheepish grin. "You know what I'd really like to have instead?"

"Just name it."

"My grandfather's steamer trunk. It'll make a perfect dresser."

I looked over at the big trunk standing open where Lainey had left it. I asked, "With or without the golf clubs."

"Without the golf clubs, but with the box of pictures."

I picked up the box of photos from the floor and pulled out the one that had captured Lainey's interest earlier, my parents together, young and in love. I showed it to her. "May I keep this one?"

"They all belong to you, Mom."

"I only want this one. I think it's time to make space for Dad on the family room wall."

Lainey looked a little suspicious. "You planning a rogue-husband gallery?"

"Not at all. I think I'll take down the portrait of your dad and send it to you. Maybe you can save a little space on the side of the table for him. And maybe some room for a little picture of your mother, too?"

"Like chaperones," she said, chuckling. "What are you going to do with the rest of the stuff in the trunk?"

"Take it home with me." What I was thinking made me feel a little bit guilty, certainly disloyal to my mother's wishes, but also stronger. I took out my father's pipe rack and sniffed it, found some remnant of the scent that had been his. "It's time for a few things to be brought back out into the open where they belong."

THE NAKED GIANT

Where California Highway One passes through Big Sur, the roadway is nothing more than a two-lane shelf cut across the face of a vertical cliff that rises straight up from the Pacific. The terrain is stark and magnificent, and treacherous. There is little margin for error on the highway. And there is no escape route once the commitment has been made.

Three times a year between the summer after my twelfth birthday and the winter before my eighteenth, I rode this natural roller coaster with my father. Christmas, Easter, and summer vacations, Dad sprung me from Saint Agnes' Preparatory School for Young Ladies in Carmel-by-Sea, and drove me south through Big Sur to Los Angeles. Even then, before there was a freeway through the inland valley, Big Sur was the long way around.

I drove the highway by myself for the first time many years after those trips with my dad. Little seemed changed. Every rainy season, chunks of the road slide into the sea hundreds of feet below. The road department bridges the gaps or cuts deeper into the cliff face, making the trip a bit more harrowing every season; the sensation is something like heading blind into the abyss. But after thirty-two winters, I still knew what I would find around every turning.

I slowed going into the curves, and punched the accelerator coming out, the way my dad taught me, letting the sideways thrust of gravity determine how fast was too fast. Pushing my husband Richard's new Mercedes to the very edge of control.

Coming out of Ragged Point, at the windingest part of the trip where the road also descends precipitously, I miscalculated the last hairpin and veered into the path of a Toyota van; sleeping bags and a tent tied to the roof, six sets of scared eyes staring at me through the windows. I yanked the wheel to the right, over-corrected. My tires — Richard's tires — ground into the shoulder, spitting gravel over the side into nothingness.

I was twenty-four inches from the edge when I stopped the car.

The jagged ridge of the Santa Lucia Range turns to the east at that point, and the terrain that lay ahead was a dramatic change from the wild Sur: rolling foothills covered with short grass, grazing cattle in the shade of liveoak trees, now and then a farm building at the base of the hills. Atop a high peak in the distance, Hearst's Castle rose from a gray mist.

"The giant's castle," my father would always say when we reached that point. Always. "And there's the giant, fat and lazy as ever, sleeping the day away under his blanket. But tonight, before the moon rises, he'll wake up and he'll be powerfully hungry. 'Little girls,' he'll bellow. 'Bring me little girls with long black ponytails for my supper.' " Then, of course, Dad would flip up my long ponytail and make disgusting ogre noises.

Later, when I was too old for Dad's stories, I saw the giant lying beside the road. I can still see him.

The round, smooth contours of California's coastal hills give the giant his human shape. His velvet blanket is the short scrub grass that burns to a soft gold during the long dry summer.

The summer I was twelve, I made the trip alone with my father for the first time. He drove a three-year-old Chrysler New Yorker. With my dad, it was always a Chrysler, but that New Yorker was a marvel: two-tone, desert pink on top, charcoal gray on the bottom, with a slash of pink along the tail fins. Eight feet of tail fins behind us. A trunk big enough to sleep a family of four.

We were a family of only three. And, shortly, not even that.

My mother hated the car, and let it be known that she wanted a new one. "Tail fins are passé, old hat, out. I'm embarrassed to be seen in that old bus."

Dad, stubborn in the face of change for change-sake, held out. A wonder of a car, he said, four-hundred-thirty-five-cubic-inch-hemi-head engine purring under the hood. He couldn't replace the car because Chrysler didn't build them like that anymore. Perfect aerodynamics, heavy body, low center of gravity, took the curves of Highway One like a dream. Like a dream.

Dad and I came out of Ragged Point onto the straight-away, driving between the ocean and the rows of rolling coastal hills, making up the usual stories about the giant and his castle. I pretended to be bored by the stories, endless variations on the giant's adventures we had made up on every trip for as long as I could remember. The only difference that time was, for the first time, my mother wasn't with us.

I pretended to be bored by the old stories, but I wasn't. And Dad knew I wasn't. And I knew he knew. That was part of the game between us that summer.

"Ach!" He pointed to cows grazing on a grassy hillside. "The old boy has fleas in his bed like a dog."

Dad laughed in a wicked way when I said that a stand of liveoak was curly hair on the giant's chest.

"Chest hair?" He was having way too much fun at my expense. "What happened to his blanket?"

I couldn't answer. I was at a particular age. The mere idea that the giant might have body hair, attractive body hair, was more than I cound think about.

We drove on in silence, or relative silence. My dad whistled the melody of "Red Sails in the Sunset" and I whistled harmony, trilling the high notes the way he taught me. I watched the landscape roll past my window at seventy-miles an hour, the hills a liquid blur of gold.

I knew that if we stopped the car and went for a walk, the ground cover would be brittle, full of stickers like nasty little foxtails that hook into your socks and work their way into your shoes and won't come out. But through the window, the grass looked smooth, translucent, delicate like the fuzz on a fresh peach held up to the sun. Or like the corner of my jaw where, in the sideview mirror, I could see downy hair in the sunlight. I put my hand against the warm window, and tried to imagine how the curve of the giant's blanket would feel. Everything I touched was deliciously smooth and warm.

The scene outside was so vast and so beautiful that my eyes could not take it all in. The scope of all that loveliness seemed to move into my chest, pressing tight like the elastic of the new bra my mother had forced upon me for the first time that very week. I knew the bra was punishment for knowing grown-up things.

My dad was still whistling. He had progressed to "Ode to Joy," and lost me after the first refrain. I listened to him, his true pitch, his elegant phrasing, while I made up my own story about the giant. This story I kept to myself because it was private, and it was scary.

The giant was no longer the grizzled ogre my dad always conjured up. The giant wasn't ugly at all anymore. And he certainly wasn't fat-bellied.

My giant was tall and slender and beautiful. His shoulder was broad, the tallest hill. The hill tapered into a valley, forming a lithe waist, then a mound rose to form his narrow hip. Rolls of land were the muscles of his long thighs.

I wanted to get the proportions just right, so I glanced down at my own skinny, sun-tanned thighs.

My eyes must have been dazzled, filled by the endless gold flying past. Because when I glanced down, my leg appeared to me to be exactly the color of the grass, and had the same downy texture. When

I looked out again at the giant's thigh, I realized that he was lying there without any blanket at all.

"He *is* naked," I whispered.

"Who is?" Dad craned his neck, looking I supposed for a tramp.

"Never mind." I hunkered down in the seat and crossed my arms over the stiff peaks formed by the hated bra. When I looked up again, the giant's leg had segued into the next series of naked shoulder, waist, then hip and thighs, followed by another and another, naked giants stretching to the horizon.

Dad tugged my ponytail. "You okay?"

"I guess."

"Then be useful. I'm ready for 'Beautiful Dreamer.' You can do the melody this time if you'll sing loud enough."

I sang with him, my hand on my bare thigh, the skin hot from the sun coming through the side window, as we passed the endless naked giants lining the highway.

Somewhere near San Luis Obispo, the song ran out. For a few moments there was no sound except the hum of the car's big motor.

"Rainey?" Dad's voice was so soft, so strange, that I sat up to see what he saw outside, expecting a red-tailed hawk in the sky — always a source for reverence. Only the same old red barn in the crook made by two round hills was out there.

"I have to pee," I said as I leaned back again, vaguely disappointed. "How much longer?"

"Can you hold it till Buellton?"

I said, "I guess."

"Rainey?"

"What?" Without much interest, I looked out again. "What do you see?"

"Listen to me." He reached across the seat and took my hand. "You're an old girl now, Rainey. You understand what makes the world go 'round."

I eyed him with suspicion. Compliments about maturity, in my experience, usually meant I was going to be hit with something I wasn't ready for. They had already told me I was going to boarding school in the fall. If there was anything worse, I didn't want to hear it.

When he took a deep breath, building courage, I said, "Oh, look. A bald eagle."

"Bald eagles are extinct."

I slouched down, glared out the window. The giant was gone: farms and fields were all around us, the barren peaks of the mountains now far off to the left.

"You know, Rainey, things between your mom and me haven't been all hunky-dory lately."

I knew what was coming, but I did nothing to help him out. I had walked in on the truth.

"Mom and I think it would be best for all of us if Mom and I take a little breather from each other. My job keeps me down in L.A. so much, we thought I might as well get a place in the city." His voice caught. "Just for a while."

"How long?" I demanded. Dad hated to make people unhappy. I knew he would let the truth out way too slowly.

That little while he mentioned was going to stretch into forever, one week at a time, or one month at a time, and he would never come right out and say in so many words what the situation really was.

He used a lot of words to avoid saying what I needed to know. "We're going to have this week, Rainey, just you and me in my new place. We'll have one helluva vacation, put our own mark on the map of the city. Then right away, after this week, school starts. You'll be so busy at Saint Agnes', getting used to a new school, you won't have time to think about your old mom and dad. Before you know it, it's Christmas. Your mother says you can spend Christmas with me. And then Easter. Turn around twice and it's summer. My new place is on the beach. Best place in the whole damn world for a kid to spend the summer."

"Hold on." I wouldn't look at him. "So, the only time I'll spend with Mom is Easter?"

"No, Rainey. You'll be with me for Easter, too."

"If I spend Christmas, Easter and summer with you, when do I stay with Mom?"

He took too long answering for me to trust what he finally said. "Weekends, when she can manage it, she'll come down to Carmel to visit you."

"But when will I go see her? When will I go home?"

"Home is in L.A. now." His smile was too big, too phony. "See, kiddo, Mom's going through something right now, and, well, her schedule isn't as set as mine is. When she wants to see you, she'll come to you."

"This is why I'm being sent to boarding school, isn't it? You're getting a divorce."

He sighed. Some unpleasant things are so obvious there's no point trying to deny them.

I had not said a single word to anyone about what I knew. But Mom knew I knew, so I had to be shipped out.

That summer, my best friend and I had spent the month of July at a camp in the Sierra Nevada. While I was away, I worried about my mother being alone all that time, because my father was down south working the entire month. I was delighted when there was some horrible bacteria found in the mountain water the camp used, and we were all sent home a couple of days early. Somehow, my mother didn't get the message. She wasn't at the airport to meet me.

When my friend's parents dropped me off at my house, the morning newspaper was still on the driveway, meaning Mom wasn't out of bed yet. As I walked in, I plotted a grand surprise entrance. I was too big to throw myself onto her bed, the way I used to. I thought about getting out my clarinet and blowing Reveille, like camp. I went to my parents' room, still thinking about how to announce myself.

Standing in the doorway, I could see my mother's outline recumbent under a soft, cream-colored blanket. Under the blanket next her, there was a second set of mounds, tangled with her like an intersecting range of hills; a long, slender, broad-shouldered form.

The summer I turned twelve, I was too young to be the by-product of a broken marriage. The summer I turned fifty, I was too old.

My husband Richard was away on business the week before my birthday. He traveled often. When he was away, when he was home for that matter, he was always considerate, always careful to reassure me that what happened to my parents would never happen to us. For my part, I made myself trust him.

Two days before my birthday, Richard called me to talk about the party he had planned to mark the end of my first half-century, payback for the five years of old-age jokes and teasing I had meted out ever since he passed that particular milestone. He said it would be a roast, but I knew that he had actually planned something quite elegant. I had overheard him talking on the telephone one day a week earlier, ordering champagne and flowers. I heard him say candlelight and satin sheets.

Richard and I lived in a townhouse in San Francisco, and used the beach cottage in Carmel I inherited from my mother for weekending; a small, romantic place she bought so that we could have weekends together when I was at school. I overheard Richard order wine and flowers to be delivered to the beach house.

How sweet he was, I thought, to plan a romantic weekend. We'd had a rocky year. To use my dad's expression, things hadn't been all hunky-dory between us. Now, here was evidence that we had crossed the rough patch.

Richard would be tired after his business trip. I wanted to surprise him by driving down to Carmel ahead, have the house aired out and the bed made before he arrived. To chill the wine.

But the wine was chilled long before I arrived.

After Ragged Point, the highway drops onto a narrow coastal plain and runs along the ocean at very nearly the surf line. During winter storms, especially when the storms coincide with the annual high tide, waves sometimes break over the highway. Motorists have been swept right out to sea.

I pulled into a turnout at San Simeon and walked down to the water, carrying a bottle of Richard's champagne. Across the road, the remnants of William Randolph Hearst's zebra herd grazed among ordinary cattle. The cows were oblivious to their exotic colleagues, but drivers now and then, seeing what cannot be there, will run right up the back of the car in front of them. Or stop dead.

There was a small sandy beach, and beyond it tide pools like gnarled fingers of black rock extended many yards out into the surf. At the far edge of the tide pools, rafts of sea otters snacked on clams and crabs, floating on their backs in a kelp bed.

I sat on the sand and drank Richard's wine and watched the otters. About halfway through the bottle I began to sing, first "Red Sails in the Sunset," then "Beautiful Dreamer." There was no one to sing harmony and I began to feel pathetic, sitting alone on the beach.

In all the years I had lived among the California hills, it had never occurred to me that the figure recumbent under the golden blanket of grass could be a woman. A giant woman. An insurmountable, endless young woman. Naked shoulders and narrow waist and round hips, long thighs, stretching to the horizon.

I did some quick arithmetic. When I walked in and found my mother in bed beside Dr. Jacks, she was thirty-two. Dr. Jacks was fifty-three. Two years younger than Richard was now.

In the soft, yellow, morning light in my parent's bedroom, when Dr. Jacks pushed the blanket aside, he did not seem old to me. He was beautiful in a way I had never expected a man to be. My dad was handsome, but he was my dad; a big, hairy, plaything. Dr. Jacks was like a marble god. All of a sudden, my perception of the world changed radically. A lot of mysteries began to make sense.

Later, when Mom admitted to the fact of Dr. Jacks, sometimes he would come with her on weekend visits to Saint Agnes'. In full sunlight, lying on the beach in his little French swim trunks, he didn't look quite so wonderful to me as he had that first morning. His skin was old, and his abdomen wasn't only flat, it was caved in, and the bulge in the front of his trunks looked weird. But that first summer, he was, to my mind, both handsome and fearsome.

Mrs. Jacks was the same age as her husband, give or take a couple of years. As were Richard and I. And the young thing making bumps under the satin sheets in my Carmel cottage? I hadn't stayed long enough to ask her age. There didn't seem much point in doing so.

Dr. Jacks and my mother lasted only a few years. After a while, she started bringing someone new when she came to visit me on weekends. I believe it was during the second man, but maybe it was during the third, that she bought the beach house near my school in Carmel. If she had to drive down regularly, she said, she might as well be comfortable. Comfort and appearances vied for pre-eminence with my mother.

Dad would have appreciated the way Richard's new Mercedes handled. A fine car on a curve. Treacherous for the bank account, but a good car for the road.

Richard and I had argued over buying the car. I thought we should pay off his last one before buying a new one. It seemed to me perfectly reasonable that a person should hang on to a luxury car as long as the engine ran beautifully and the body was in reasonable condition. I guess that, like my father, I misunderstood what it was that made new better.

The last trip I took with my father through Big Sur was the June I graduated from Saint Agnes'. Dad was unusually quiet all the way down the coast. We sang, as always, but he didn't have much to say. By that year, he had gone through two more Chryslers. Not one of them gave him a fraction of the pleasure the old charcoal and desert rose New Yorker had, but he remained faithful to the maker.

There had been in turn a green one and a white one, and finally a coffee-brown one. The last Chrysler was wide and boxy, too long in the wheel base to hold the road, and it was incredibly ugly. Didn't corner worth a damn. The engine was so tricked out with pollution control devices that it had no acceleration. Felt like a turtle, Dad said as the big car rocked and swayed through curves. Worst of all, it was no fun to drive.

I had one last, hot summer in Los Angeles. Years before, we had moved from the beach to a house built on stilts overhanging Coldwater Canyon. I never liked the isolation in the canyon, though my father seemed to crave it. I looked for any excuse to stay away.

That summer after high school, I avoided Dad, the way young people headed out into the world avoid their parents. Dad and I rarely saw each other. I had a job as lifeguard at the local kiddie pool, and that kept me away from home all day. Evenings I spent with a boyfriend, a surfer I dumped the night before I flew east for college.

If my father was unhappy during those months, I did not bother to notice.

Over the years after the divorce, there was a steady erosion of Dad's high spirits. I attributed his growing quietude to his age, the pressures of business, the smog that filled his canyon nearly every afternoon, the emptiness of his house when I wasn't there, the noise when I was. I never worried about him.

I got the call from my mother about halfway through my first college semester. Dad had driven his newest Chrysler, the coffee-brown one, up the coast highway to Big Sur. Just north of Lucia — guest cabins and a diner were the town — where the highway is three-hundred feet above the ocean, his car left the road.

"Miscalculated a curve," Mom said. "He always drove too damn fast."

I had driven that road with Dad enough times that I knew she was wrong. The only curve in his entire life he ever miscalculated was my mother.

Divers retrieved Dad's body from the ocean floor, but they couldn't bring up the car. They were, however, able to answer one question for me: there hadn't been a blow-out. A flat tire was the only variable I wondered about.

I poured the flat remains of Richard's champagne into the tide pools and carried the empty bottle with me back to the Mercedes. The big birthday party was tomorrow. I needed to tell my children not to come, that the party was off. Richard had the car's cell phone with him at the cottage: how easy he made it for me to reach him anywhere, anytime he was out of town, no bother with hotel desk clerks. I headed back north, looking for a telephone.

A busload of tourists was just unloading at the general store at San Simeone. I didn't want to wade through a lot of people to use the public phone. I didn't want strangers to see me if I started to cry. Instead, I drove on to Lucia.

All the way up, I imagined my father making his last trip alone in that car that he resented. I tried to sing "Ode to Joy," imitating Dad's phrasing, but gave it up. I never could sing or whistle as well as he did.

Lucia is nothing more than a turnout with a few parking places on the ocean side of the highway. An old log-cabin restaurant hangs out over the water there. Below the restaurant, a narrow wooden stairway courses down the face of the cliff, branching off to a dozen or so tiny guest cottages. The cottages have few amenities, but the view of the water three-hundred feet straight down is incomparable.

The lot in front of the restaurant was full, so I drove on to the first turn-out and parked there, though the space was narrow and the side of the car was too close to the highway. I decided to trust the skill of drivers coming around the bend, because, more than anything at that moment, I needed coffee from the restaurant before I spoke with my son and daughter. Wine had left me light headed, had made it impossible to push away the picture of Richard rising naked from the bed. My bed.

At the exact spot where my father went over the side, the guardrail was missing. Someone had hit it, or had gone right through it, but who could say when? The broken edges of the metal rail were rusty; a tribute to the sorry shape of the state's highway budget.

I walked to the edge and looked down. Then I picked up a boulder and threw it out as far away from the bluff as I could. It seemed to hang on the air, and then, silently, dropped against the rocks sticking out of the ocean far below and disappeared.

If a car drops into the sea and no one is there to hear it, does it make a noise?

My children and their spouses had booked flights into San Francisco the following morning. I called my daughter in Seattle and my son in Denver and left messages on their machines. "Don't bother to come. I've decided not to turn fifty after all. The party is off. I'll call you when I get home."

I was glad no one was at either home to ask the requisite questions. What could I say to the kids? I shouldn't have argued with Richard about a new car? I shouldn't have let myself become last year's model? With my family history, I should have seen it coming?

A car pulled out of the restaurant lot and left an open space. I went back for the Mercedes, relieved to have a safer place to park. What would I say to Richard if someone side-swiped his investment?

I started Richard's Mercedes, felt the power of its big engine rumbling under the hood. I waited for a car, then a motorcycle, to pass, and then eased onto the highway. I can't say exactly what happened next. I was thinking about the many times Dad and I had stopped in Lucia for hot cocoa or cold lemonade, depending on the school holiday. I remembered when we stopped the day he drove me to Saint Agnes' after our first summer vacation in Los Angeles.

Dad had almost cried when it was time to get back into the car for the last leg of the trip: he was moving me in to boarding school and continuing on to remove the last of his things from the house he had shared with my mother.

Dr. Jacks had already taken over Dad's dresser and closet, and Dad's half of the cream-colored blanket on the bed. The reason I was not allowed to go to that house on weekends to stay with my mother was the adulterous presence of Dr. Jacks within her walls.

As I turned the Mercedes onto the highway, Richard's empty champagne bottle rolled from under the seat and bumped my ankle. Maybe that little nudge was the trigger. It occurred to me that if the bottle had rolled under the brake pedal, say, or under my foot, it could have made me lose control of the car. I could have slipped over the edge, just the way my father had.

When that empty bottle rolled against my leg, all cold and hard, for just a bare instant I thought about what might happen if I drove into the silence beyond the broken guardrail. No one would know what happened to me, anymore than we ever knew what happened to Dad.

Maybe the divers who went down for me would come up with the empty bottle, giving people a wrong idea. A somewhat wrong idea, at any rate.

And Richard? I couldn't trust him to say, "I ripped Rainey's heart out of her chest by sleeping with another woman, incidentally a younger woman, on the very eve of my wife's birthday. *Mea Culpa. Mea culpa. Mea Maxima Culpa.*"

I knew Richard would let me take the long plunge all by myself. With that realization, at last I was furious with him. If I went over the edge, I wanted everyone to know exactly why. But why should I be the one to go over the edge?

The road ahead rose slightly, and then, going into the curve, descended. If the wheels of Richard's Mercedes were set straight — what wonderful steering the Mercedes had — and were headed against the angle of the banked road, and if the champagne bottle was wedged against the accelerator when the car was popped into drive, the car's low center of gravity and perfect alignment would keep it on a true course as it came off the rise. The car should go straight across the curve, over the narrow gravel shoulder, right between the rusted edges of the broken guard rail and over the edge, motor still humming as it dove straight off into nothing.

At a window table in the Lucia restaurant, I had two cups of coffee and a turkey sandwich. While the waitress, a cheerful woman who loved a healthy appetite, prepared for me a slice of homemade apple pie a la mode, I went to the telephone beside the front counter and called Richard's cell phone. How long had it been since I allowed myself to eat a piece of pie a la mode?

"Jesus, Rainey, honey. What can I say? I'm so sorry. She's nothing to me. Nothing. I can't explain. It was something that just happened."

"Something that just happened?" I thought about the phone calls he made, all the preparations for the tryst: candles and wine, flowers and satin sheets. "Just happened the way a car wreck just happens?"

"Where are you, Rainey? Come home. We have to talk."

"Actions speak louder than ..."

"Are you all right?"

"I'm fine, all things considered. Tomorrow is my birthday and I'll be older than dirt. And I'll be alone." I returned the waitress' wave when she set my pie at my place. "I've called the children and told them not to come tomorrow. I'll leave all the others to you. I can't imagine what you'll say to everyone."

"I'll just say you're under the weather."

"In that case, I'll make the calls."

The waitress whispered to me as she swept by, "That pie's real hot. Don't let the ice cream all melt if you want the good of it."

"Rainey, honey."

"Richard, don't call anyone. I've decided that I want to go ahead with the party. Please don't think you have to come. In fact, don't come. I'll make your excuses."

"I can't blame you for being upset."

"I'm not upset," I said. "At least, not anymore. I have to go now. My dessert is ready. I have just enough time to finish it before the car rental people from San Luis Obispo get here to pick me up."

"Car rental? Where the hell is my car?"

"Exactly," I said. "Where the hell is your car?"

I ate as much of the pie as I wanted. When I was finished, I waited out in front of the restaurant until the car rental people came and fetched me. All the way down the highway to San Luis Obispo, the young driver and I shared stories about the giant who slept under the gold velvet blanket. When I told him the giant was naked, the kid already knew.

"So," I asked him, "can you sing harmony?"

"Sure," he said. "If you don't sing too loud."

THE LAST IS ADORATION

Nancy awoke, as usual, fifteen minutes before Walt's alarm went off. The bedroom was frigid because Walt liked to sleep with a window open, even if there was snow falling outside, as there was that Friday morning.

How nice it would be, just this once, Nancy thought, to snuggle down into the delicious warmth under the quilt and go back to sleep for another few minutes. Or for half an hour or half a day: it wasn't as if she had to be anywhere until the Three Angel A's luncheon meeting in the church basement at noon.

The thought of her meeting impelled Nancy upward. Today was her turn to give a progress report and she had plenty to say. The opening phrase would begin, "I gazed down upon my sleeping angel this morning and ..."

Nancy had to take a look at Walt for inspiration before she could finish her opening. She raised up on one elbow, holding down the quilt so that Walt wouldn't feel a gush of chilly air, and gazed at him over his shoulder. His face was smooshed into his pillow, his mouth hung open. As he snored softly, a crusty line of drool ran down his stubbley chin and onto the starched, ironed pillowcase. Strangely, the toenails of the foot he dangled out of the covers — she had to lean all the way over him to make sure that what she saw wasn't a trick of the morning light — were painted with clear nail polish. The temptation was huge to wake him just to hear how he would explain away nail polish. But she fought the urge and beat it.

Not pretty, her Walt, she mused as she studied him. A good provider certainly, but not handsome. Or kind. Or affectionate. Or ...

123

Nancy stopped herself before she got further into her old sin of fault finding. She had made a new commitment to her life with Walt based on the Angel As' three-part vow. She would accept Walt, whatever his flaws. She would accommodate herself to his interests and desires as if they were she own. And last, she promised to adore him until death parted them.

Adoring Walt took greater strength than accepting or accommodating did. The effort it took to adore, however, gave her a sense of accomplishment and pride.

Nancy reached for her pale-rose silk peignoir as she slipped out from under the comforter. Her old flannel robe would have been more comfortable against the frigid morning, but what if Walt woke up and saw her in it, all lumpy and frayed looking? The first step toward the last vow — adoration of spouse — was making herself worthy of adoration in return.

In the bathroom with the door closed so that the light wouldn't disturb Walt, Nancy washed her face and applied make-up; light make-up for early morning. Then she brushed and sprayed her short hair and when she was as adorable as she could be so early, she walked through a spritz of Walt's favorite perfume.

Walt was particular about the way things smelled. Some perfumes gave him a headache. This particular scent was one to which Walt had given rare approval after sniffing it on the neck of a restaurant hostess. Nancy had, at his request, bought this same scent for him to give his secretary at Christmas. She thought that perfume was a rather personal gift for a boss to give a young female employee, but better to risk crossing the line of propriety than to have her husband come home mid-day with a migraine. And she didn't like the scent very much. It was too earthy for her taste. But she wore it daily to please Walt. Accommodation was, after all, the second step.

When the alarm went off, Nancy was in the kitchen whipping up a vegetable omelet made with egg substitute. The aroma of bran muffins baking filled the room. The orange juice she squeezed by hand because the sound of the electric reamer annoyed him, was on the table, iced and ready.

Walt walked in just as the muffins came out of the oven.

"Good morning, my love," she cooed as she presented herself to him for a kiss. The silk peignoir billowed behind her, the lightest aura of scent embraced her; Walt did not.

"Morning." Walt slurped from the coffee cup she placed in his hand.

"How handsome you look today, as everyday." Nancy pulled out a chair for him at the kitchen table. A single rose from her greenhouse rested beside his juice glass. "Your breakfast is ready, darling."

Walt looked between the pan on the stove and the carton of egg substitute on the counter and sniffed disapprovingly. "How many times do I have to tell you, I hate that fake egg gunk. You want to make me an omelet, crack something that's passed through a real chicken before you pass it on to me."

"Dr. Gray says we should look after our cholesterol."

"Then feed that phony crap to the Doc." Still standing, he swallowed his juice in a single gulp. "I'm not hungry."

"You have such a long day ahead, dear." She held up the basket of hot bran muffins. "At least take a muffin."

He scowled at the muffins. "I'll get something on my way into town."

In the old days, Nancy would have snapped at Walt, told him what a fussy prick he was and warned him that he would die a young man if he didn't eat what she knew was good for him. But that sort of screed ended when she embraced the Three Angel A's. She had graduated from step one, Acceptance, a full month ago. If Walt was cranky, she knew now that the fault was hers for not accepting his preferences as her own.

Or was this an accommodation situation? Sometimes she felt all muddled on the differences between those two A's. Whatever, tomorrow Walt could have anything he wanted for breakfast. And, blessedly, she now knew exactly what she would say at the meeting today when it was her turn to deliver testimonial.

Taking pride that she had overcome both hurt feelings and the temptation to scold, Nancy walked ahead of Walt to the front door. She picked up his briefcase and held it out to him with a serene — she hoped — smile on her face while he put on his overcoat.

"Have a lovely day, my dear," she said, her voice sweet with adoration.

"Uh huh," Walt said. He gave her a perfunctory kiss on the lips, which she accepted; Walt was never a morning person.

"What time shall I have dinner ready?" she asked as he took his briefcase from her.

"Dunno," he shrugged. "I may fly down to Chicago for a meeting. I'll call you if I stay over."

She stopped herself from clenching her fists. "Have a blessed day, darling."

He grunted something that she chose to hear as "I love you."

After Walt was gone, Nancy was ready to clean. She changed from her peignoir into jeans and one of Walt's cast-off dress shirts, took her supply basket from the pantry, and, beginning upstairs, scrubbed her way down to the front door. By eleven o'clock every surface sparkled, the laundry was washed, ironed and put away. For her special project of the day, she relined and reorganized Walt's sock drawer as a way to fight down the image of his shiny toenails.

Last thing before she went upstairs to shower and dress for the luncheon meeting, Nancy unwrapped the three snapshots she had picked up from the framers the day before: Walt with his airplane, Walt with his fishing boat, Walt in his office with his secretary standing beside him.

Acceptance, accommodation, adoration — the photographs represented all three. Small planes scared her, boats made her seasick, the secretary couldn't type. Accept, accommodate, adore, she repeated a couple of times as she arranged the framed photographs on the entry hall table so that, first thing when he walked in, Walt would feel the blessing of all three Angel A's.

As she walked upstairs, Nancy was hit by inspiration: there was a container of homemade potato-leek soup in the freezer. If Walt was flying his plane down to Chicago in this cold weather, a Thermos of hot soup would doubtless be welcome.

✣ ✣

Afternoons, Elva Lovelace's downtown nail parlor offered a businessman's two-for-the-price-of-one lunchtime pedicure special. Elva's idea, and a fine one, she thought, was to persuade the gray-suit crowd that good grooming and good business went hand in hand. Or, foot in hand, as it were.

If men could pee standing next to each other, surely they wouldn't quail at side-by-side grooming. Besides, what better place could there be for two men to talk business uninterrupted than seated side by side for an hour in comfy leather chairs while Elva and her assistant, Carol, sliced off calluses, creamed cracked heels and trimmed and buffed masculine toenails?

Elva converted an unused storage room near the salon's back door into a pleasant private parlor for this service, and furnished it in her interpretation of masculine preference. She made arrangements for a sandwich shop to make deliveries and installed a fax machine for the new clientele.

She had expected pairs of forward-thinking executives to fill the appointment book. As it turned out, the pairs who came into Elva's parlor for tandem pedicures were usually secretaries taking long lunch breaks, and not the bosses for whom the offer was intended. Now and again, the secretaries returned with their boyfriends. Sometimes those boyfriends were also their bosses. A mini-fridge stocked with wine was installed next to the fax machine and Elva would wait at the back door for the discreet souls who preferred to enter through the alley.

Friday turned out to be an unusually busy morning. The winter formal at the local high school was scheduled for that evening. Elva suspected that half the girls in the senior class had ditched classes so they could get their nails and hair done. When her regular noon hour pedicure appointment didn't show, she was so caught up in the fun of formal preparations that the appointed time for her tandem had long passed before she noticed.

Just as well the regular hadn't come, she thought when she got around to checking the appointment book. First, the parlor didn't lose any money because she and Carol had each finished two extra manicures during that hour, thereby also easing some of the crowding in the small reception area. Next, though the man was a good tipper and had referred some of his influential friends to her, there were times when his behavior in her back room with his henna-rinsed secretary made Elva, as the proprietor, feel a little cheap. The way the secretary would just reach up under her short skirt and pull off her panty hose in front of her boss and Carol and Elva, and the way he made his wife the butt of cruel jokes — telling one and all, for instance that his wife starched and ironed his boxers and arranged them in his drawer by color — were not in keeping with the high-toned ambience Elva envisioned when she first made her two-for-the-price-of-one offering.

THE LAST IS ADORATION

❖ ❖

Everyone knew you could set your watch by Nancy Mayhand. If the Three Angel A's called a meeting for noon, then by noon Nancy would have her contribution to the buffet luncheon set on the table with serving utensils at the ready, flowers from her greenhouse arranged and placed in vases, herself refreshed from a visit to the powder room and in her seat, prepared to offer her testimony.

On occasion a lady in the group might make a less-than-kind joke about Nancy's precision in all things. Nancy would shrug off any such remark as envy on the part of some less organized sister Angel. There was something a little bit scary about Nancy: a brittleness that barely covered her despair. She had so much energy and so much drive, if she snapped ...

On Friday at five minutes after noon, when Nancy had still not arrived, Mrs. Lipcott, the minister's wife, placed a call to the Mayhand home.

"No answer," Mrs. Lipcott announced when she returned to the ladies waiting in the basement. Sally Orchard started to say how nice it would be, for once, not to have Nancy dominate a meeting, but the look of genuine concern on Mrs. Lipcott's face stopped her. The minister's wife said, "I should call Walt."

❖ ❖

Shep Huey was supposed to cover the office when his boss was at lunch. But Friday was a slow day. The boss, Walt Mayhand, never called in during his lunch hour on Fridays, so no one would know if Shep took off early. On that Friday, the boss had disappeared at ten minutes before noon. And who knew where Walt's secretary was?

At 12:20 Friday, Shep was sneaking out, using the private back stairwell of the Mayhand Office Tower, when he ran across the broken thermos halfway down. A building four stories tall didn't exactly make a "tower," to Shep's way of thinking. But the boss's wife had big ideas. Towering ideas, you might say. When she set her mind to something, Shep and the boss and everyone else had learned it was best just to go along. Considering all the grand ideas the woman had had over the years, giving an inappropriate name to a building was small potatoes.

Potatoes, Shep sniffed. That's what he smelled. Potatoes. The soup oozing out around the broken Thermos looked like tomato, or maybe beet, but it smelled like potato. And there was a lot of it. Who would think that a little two-cup thermos could make such a big, red mess?

Feeling put upon, feeling hungry — the soup smelled wonderful; earthy, feral — Shep lumbered back up the stairs to summon the janitor to come and clean up the mess. Maybe he chiseled on his time card, but Shep was a man of genuinely good character. He would not want anyone to slip and get hurt, even if he had to sacrifice some of his own stolen time to take care of the housekeeping.

❧ ❧

Carla Pellagio sat in the cockpit of Walt's Leer jet, waiting. She had given up trying to retouch her week-old manicure. It was so cold that the polish just clumped up when she tried to brush it on. For this, she blamed Walt.

He had thrust their weekend bags on her and told her to call and cancel their weekly nail appointment because at the last minute "something came up." He would take care of business and be right along, he said. So, here she sat, coat buttoned all the way, her cashmere scarf, a gift from Walt, wrapped around her ears, ruining her hair. And still she froze: Walt liked her to wear skirts. Little itty-bitty skirts.

As soon as Walt showed up, Carla vowed, she would let him have it. She had decided that it was time for him to define for her why she should put up with so much discomfort for him. She had lugged both of their weekend bags down the back stairwell and out of the office and stowed them in the jet. She had made the hotel reservations in Chicago. And the dinner reservations, and bought the theater tickets, and ordered the wine he liked to be sent up to their room. Oh yes, and stopped on her way to the little executive airstrip to buy some new lingerie. For Walt. Everything to make it easier for Walt to spend time with her away from the prying eyes of everyone in town. As soon as he dumped that wife of his and made good on his promises ...

Suddenly Carla remembered that she had forgotten to call and cancel their regular nail appointment with Elva. She checked her Rolex: too late. It was already 12:30. By now, Elva knew Carla and Walt weren't coming.

Monday morning, when they were back from Chicago, Carla would send Elva a check and some flowers so that Elva wouldn't give away their regular Friday appointment. That weekly pedicure session, and the post-pedicure session at Carla's downtown apartment, were the cement that kept Walt committed to her.

Carla checked her watch again. Walt was never late. He had told her five minutes. When she arrived at the airstrip, because she had stopped at La La Lingerie, she had expected him to be waiting for her — flight plan submitted, pre-flight check list finished.

Carla pulled her scarf tight around her throat. Where was Walt?

❖ ❖

Shortly after 12:30, Nancy Mayhand walked into the church basement. Her face was flushed; it was cold outside. A light snow had begun to fall.

Half of the Angels had already filled their plates from the buffet table and found seats at the long refectory tables arranged to form a large U, the other half was still in line. Nancy looked at her friends, all of them looking back at her, and then shrugged, as if resigned that they had not waited for her before they began serving. She set her

Italian tomato-burger casserole among the hot foods, not even bothering to stir the obviously cold and congealing meat mixture at the edges of the bowl into the warmer center. There was no spill of winter roses in her arms, no vases. Nancy merely chonked a big serving spoon into the mass of meat and pasta and then took her place at the end of buffet the line.

All of the Angels watched this entry, all of them silent, agog. Only Mrs. Lipcott, the minister's wife, who always served herself last, walked over and put an arm around Nancy's thin shoulders.

"I was beginning to worry, dear," Mrs. Lipcott said. "Are the roads icy? Were you held up?"

"The roads? No." At first Nancy seemed distracted. Distraught, perhaps, as she clutched one of the church's thick pottery plates to her chest. Then, slowly, Nancy focussed on Mrs. Lipcott's face. She smiled. She looked down at the plate. She relaxed. "It wasn't the roads that were icy."

Mrs. Lipcott gave Nancy a gentle pat on the shoulder. "Fill your plate, then find a seat. I'll bring coffee to you, dear."

Nancy caught Mrs. Lipcott's hand as the older woman turned toward the coffee urn.

"My dear?" Mrs. Lipcott raised her brow.

Nancy extended her empty plate toward the minister's wife.

"Thank you, Mrs. Lipcott, but I'm not staying today."

Mrs. Lipcott looked from the plate to the parishioner's perfectly made-up face. "Are you ill?"

"No. I'm fine." Nancy surveyed the semi-circle of expectant faces staring at her; there was precious little friendship among them. "It's just that I have no testimony to give today. I accepted, I accommodated, I tried to adore. I'm tired, Mrs. Lipcott. And I have absolutely nothing left to say."

Nancy turned and walked out of the church basement.

THE LAST IS ADORATION

After Nancy Mayhand left, Mrs. Lipcott noticed that she had left a trail of tomato sauce. Perhaps some of her casserole had spilled and Nancy had walked through it. Mrs. Lipcott was afraid that someone might slip on the red sauce; everyone knew how thick Nancy's sauces were. She moistened a paper towel and began to wipe up the footprints, working her way toward the door.

It was well past her usual lunchtime, and the minister's wife was hungry. Nancy was such a wonderful cook. Even if Nancy Mayhand could be challenging, demanding, self-involved, Mrs. Lipcott would miss her buffet contributions.

The aroma wafting up from the towel was spicy, earthy. Feral. Mrs. Lipcott was reminded of the perfume her husband had asked her to buy for the church secretary at Christmas.

THE SKY SHALL BE BLUE

Tuesday evening, late. Pouring rain. Cars slipping and sliding on slick pavement. "Like bumper cars," Lettie groused, adding a muttered, "If people can't remember how to drive from one storm to the next then they should stay home. It's not as if it *never* rains in California. Idiots!" There was no one in the car with her to hear and appreciate what she knew were entirely valid complaints, but she felt better for having said them aloud.

Lettie felt like grousing about a lot of things that Tuesday evening besides bad drivers. Her wet clothes, her car's inadequate window defogger, her nearly-out-of-control splurge at Nordstroms, all took a verbal hit or two. It didn't help her foul frame of mind that the big iron gate across her condo's underground-garage ramp was slow and balky when she tapped the remote opener. She had to wait, in the downpour with her fogged-up windows, longer than she thought appropriate. Lettie, who had served one term on the condo's board of directors, knew how much was spent for gate maintenance. For the cost, the gate should move quickly and smoothly.

"We'll get the service we pay for," she said, feeling almost exultant as she began to compose her complaint. "Good service, or heads will roll."

"Heads will roll." She liked the way that sounded, so she said it again, quite loud this time and rolled the R for emphasis. Aware, belatedly, that there might be neighbors in the garage who could see her declaiming to no one, she stomped on her brakes and took a good look around, ready to hop out and confront anyone who might later gossip about Lettie talking to herself. Her fists balled up reflexively, the way they used to when she would face down kids on the playground to make them shut up.

Lettie glanced at her tight little fists and immediately heard her mother's reproach: "Don't get yourself into a snit over nothing." Merely thinking about her mother dredged up a substantial cache of old, unresolved grievances, usually concerning Lettie's insistence that rules should be followed and infractions reported. Had Lettie not been correct to challenge the first prize Ralphy Hallmeyer received for a landscape painting in which he painted the sky green? Skies are blue. Everyone knows skies are blue. Everyone except colorblind people like Ralphy. She conceded that his picture was the prettiest, but it should have been disqualified because his sky wasn't a sky, it was some green mass. But was he disqualified? No. Ralphy got first prize and Lettie got nothing except sent home from school, where, insult to injury, her mother sent her straight to her room to think things over. The incident happened years ago, in the fifth grade, but the injustice of its outcome still stung Lettie like a fresh punch in the eye.

"Skies are blue," Lettie grumbled as she began to pull Nordstroms bags out of the back seat. "Always blue."

There were so many bags. Lettie hadn't realized as she tumbled the bags into her car a few at a time just how many bags there were. She felt a surge of panic when she thought about having to defend the necessity for every single purchase the moment she walked through her front door with her arms full, again. Preparing herself for a good scolding was also a reflex. As she reached for her third bag she reminded herself that, with Mother gone and husband gone, there was no one left to complain about any damn thing she did, said, or bought. At last, she felt a breeze through the black shroud of her anger.

Lettie took a deep, cleansing breath. The only challenge ahead was figuring out how to get all of her purchases upstairs in one trip. As she gathered the bags, she caught little glimpses of her lovely new things all nestled among leaves of tissue paper. Each peek lifted her spirits. Two hanging-garment bags and five big handled bags weren't so horrible for one shopping excursion, she decided. Could have been much worse. On occasion, had been much worse. Just the same, she gave herself a gentle little lecture and made a promise to stick to a budget from now on.

With all of her purchases balanced in her arms, Lettie started off across the vast, well-lit expanse of the garage. She was a bit lost in reverie, imagining which of her new outfits she would wear to work the next day, imagining what her co-workers would say or the envy they might feel, when a racket of shopping cart wheels alerted her that she wasn't alone in the huge garage. She stopped to see who else was there because she generally found it best to avoid certain neighbors with whom she had unpleasant history. When she saw that the "other" was the new neighbor, a woman whom she had not yet met, she again took a deep breath and relaxed.

The new neighbor, pushing a shopping cart, stopped to collect her mail from the rank of boxes next to the elevator anteroom. The woman was about Lettie's age, attractive and well dressed, lived alone; a professional woman, like Lettie.

Lettie, who was a person who noticed things, noticed that, for a woman who lived alone, the neighbor certainly bought a lot of groceries. Maybe she entertains, Lettie thought. Lettie dared to hope that after they actually met, maybe the woman would invite Lettie to one of her entertainments. Maybe the two of them would become friends. Sharing dinners in each other's homes, going to movies, or maybe even concerts together. If Lettie could let the woman know her for her real self before the condo biddies had a chance to poison the possibilities, maybe ...

Lettie began to compose a nice personal introduction. Her load was bulky and heavy and she felt awkward trying to keep a grip on it all. Again she reproached herself: Why had she bought so much? She must look like a fool, struggling with her stuff, bedraggled after her dash through the rain at the mall. What sort of first impression would she make with her wet hair, muddy shoes and sodden coat, and all this evidence of self-indulgence?

Lettie decided to wait for another time to introduce herself. Lettie hung back, let the neighbor collect her mail, unlock the door to the elevator anteroom and wheel her grocery cart over the annoyingly high sill. She watched until the door had closed again before she moved forward.

An uncomfortable thought occurred to her: Though Lettie had never met the newcomer, the newcomer had obviously met some of the other condo residents. The clue: the newcomer knew to find grocery carts inside the rubbish room next to the mailboxes. Lettie hoped that whoever revealed this bit of information also cautioned that protocol called for residents to return the carts to the rubbish room immediately after use. It was a pet peeve of Lettie that some people merely shoved their empty carts into the elevator when it was upstairs, expecting the next person going down to put them away. Or, worse, left carts outside the elevator. Who did they think would put the carts away?

Like a flash, Lettie's hopefulness about a friendship with the new neighbor faded. Whoever told the woman where to find carts would doubtless have told her a few other things, as well.

With a heavy heart, Lettie collected the mail from her box; bills, for the most part. She hiked the slick plastic garment bags higher on her shoulder and managed to unlock the heavy anteroom door, called the elevator, pushed the button for the first floor. She stepped out of the elevator into a downpour. All the jostling to get out her keys and hold on to her mail, simply walking, had disarranged her acquisitions. The big garment bags hung heavily, and everything was getting wet.

"Quite a load." Upstairs, the new neighbor, sheltered under an umbrella, emptied shopping cart beside her, waited for the elevator down. She smiled at Lettie. "Need a hand?"

Embarrassed, flustered, Lettie managed to smile and say, "No thank you," as she scurried by. "I can manage."

"Quite a storm," the woman said to her back. She sounded friendly and warm.

"Is it ever," Lettie said. She hunkered down against the rain and hurried toward home. Behind her, she heard the cart's wheels bump over the elevator door rails, heard the elevator door close. She took a deep and happy breath, daring to hope again that the woman had possibilities. The new neighbor seemed lovely and friendly, and, best of all, she knew to take her cart back down to its rightful place in the rubbish room.

Lettie paused for a moment and considered waiting for the woman to come back up, and then introducing herself properly. However, what she heard next chilled her to the very core of her hopefulness.

"We haven't met."

Lettie wheeled.

"I'm Carlisle Jones." The neighbor extended her hand toward Lettie and smiled. "Friends call me Carlie. I just moved into unit six."

The cart was in the elevator. And Carlisle Jones wasn't. Worse yet, Carlisle Jones could see perfectly well that Lettie didn't have a free hand to shake. Could it be that the gesture was a taunt, a reproach for the shopping splurge? Had a neighbor said something to her already, like why Lettie wasn't elected to a second term on the condo association board of directors? Lettie's hands, even though they were full, began to form little fists.

"So you're the one who's always leaving carts in the elevator," Lettie snapped. "You're driving us all crazy, leaving carts all over the place."

"I'm sorry." The proffered hand dropped. Carlisle Jones looked chagrined, confused. "I left my elevator key inside. Just this once ..."

"Who do you think puts the carts away when you don't?" Rivulets of rainwater poured down Lettie's face, but she held her ground to say what needed to be said to the neighbor from unit six. The neighbor met Lettie's glare with a blank expression, just stood there under her umbrella and stared.

Lettie said, "Carts go back downstairs to the rubbish room, period."

The reproach was met with silence.

"Your mother doesn't live here," was Lettie's parting shot as she turned away and, hunkered into her drenched coat, strode toward her own front door. She might have heard a little snicker behind her, but couldn't be sure. Inside her home, the only sounds she heard were the steady downpour outside and the heavy breathing inside her chest.

Lettie put away her things, showered, nuked a frozen dinner and sat down in front of the television to eat. The encounter with Carlisle Jones had robbed her of appetite. Never since her husband moved out had she felt so keenly alone; Carlisle Jones was in many ways her last hope among her neighbors. Feeling restless and possibly remorseful, she set aside the low-fat veggie lasagna, put on a slicker and went out for a short, brisk walk around the condo grounds to clear her mind.

Lettie's first stop was the elevator, hoping Carlisle Jones had redeemed herself. Perhaps Jones cared what Lettie thought about maintaining order and had put her cart away in the rubbish room. But Lettie found that Carlisle Jones's cart was exactly where she left it, as well as another. Lettie pulled out both carts and wheeled them to the patio gate outside unit six. At first she parked the carts across the gate, blocking it. Then, after some thought, she opened the gate and pushed both carts into Carlisle Jones's patio. Surely, here was a message that would not be missed: carts that are not put away become a nuisance.

Feeling she had delivered a powerful warning that carelessness would not go unnoticed, Lettie strolled on. The rain had abated, and only a fine cold mist fell on her slicker. All was quiet for the most part. But not for the entire part: she paused to listen outside unit eight where Leo the jazz saxophonist lived. There had been several occasions when his music could be heard several units away. The condo rules were clear: "No domestic noise shall be discernible outside any unit after ten PM." By standing very still and listening very carefully, she was just able to hear faint but discernible strains of music. Her watch said ten-fifteen.

Lettie made a mental note. Noise complaint number three against unit eight would be mailed first thing in the morning. Complaint number three would carry a fine. Even though Lettie was no longer on the condo association board of directors, she would make sure the complaint was placed on the agenda. A rule, after all, was there to be enforced.

Before she returned to her own quiet, orderly unit, Lettie made several other mental notes. There was a table on the patio outside unit thirteen that was not standard patio furniture. Lettie'd had to stand on a planter to see it, but see it she did. And Old Mr. Edwards had left a trash bag outside his front door. "Trash shall be appropriately deposited in the rubbish room." The rules did not excuse old men on crutches on rainy nights. Making similar notes, she made her way from one end of the development to the other.

She forewent reporting the dog in unit three even though the rule was that no dogs over thirty pounds were allowed. The little pooch looked like he had recently put on some weight and was probably over the thirty-pound limit, but his owner greeted Lettie every morning as he set out for his walk. Daily walks said to her that the owner was dealing with the weight problem. Besides, by the time Lettie had looped past unit three she was headed home, and her head was full enough of broken rules that had to be mended that an overweight dog complaint would be overkill.

After she wrote her letters, Lettie slept the sleep of the just. She faced the new day feeling refreshed and optimistic. First of all, she had something new to wear every day for the rest of the week, and, second, she had done her best to make certain that the value of her property was not eroded by the carelessness of her neighbors. Lettie felt so well that morning, that she decided to make her rounds a regular, nightly event instead of the occasional foray, as had been her habit. On her way home from work that night, she stopped and bought a pocket-sized notebook that would serve as a daily log.

Five infraction letters reached the office of the condo manager two days later. Each complaint was well-phrased, and each cited the exact infraction as defined by the association rules. And, of course, a signed copy of each complaint was stuffed into the mailbox of every resident. Six letters arrived the day after, seven the day after that. The significance of half the subsequent letters was that none of the earlier infractions was immediately remedied. She could, even if just barely, hear music from unit eight every single night. A certain non-conforming patio table was still there, carts did not get put away, and so on. After two weeks of diligence, Lettie found that sloppiness and violations still abounded. Indeed, it seemed to her that there were more infractions to report every single day.

From her first night out Lettie, who was indeed a person who noticed things, began to notice the frequency of infractions of other sorts. On evening number nine she began to keep two logs. Trash and carts and noise violations, and other public nuisances, she recorded on the front pages of her notebook. The other violations, the private ones, she recorded on the back pages. Lettie noticed that every time Mr. Oliver in unit four, a professor of geology, was away on weekend fieldtrips with students, Mrs. Oliver had overnight "guests." Arthur

Cain, who was frequently sloppy when he disposed of his trash, routinely doctored the original hotel receipts from his business trips so that he claimed an extra three days on his expense account. Lettie knew this because on one weekend when he was supposed to be in Cleveland he was at home, in the pool with his wife; during that time, Lettie logged an infraction when he hung a wet pool towel over a balcony rail. Carlisle Jones, who had moved from out-of-state, did not register her car with the Department of Motor Vehicles within thirty days of establishing residence. Young Mike Evers had a habit of sneaking out at night to smoke dope with some other youths behind the corner service station. The daughter of the old woman who had died a year ago in unit twelve was still receiving, and depositing, her mother's Social Security checks. The married gardener let his boyfriend — his boyfriend — live in unit five, a vacant unit the gardener was paid to take care of. And so on.

As a matter of duty, Lettie routinely sent letters of information to the people affected by the second set of violations. She was certain they all would be grateful. A copy was also always sent to the violator, because that was the fair thing to do. Within days of receiving notice, Mrs. Oliver moved out, Mr. Cain was looking for a new job, and young Mike was on restriction. The gardener had moved into unit five *and* had quit weeding the flowerbed outside Lettie's unit. Just punishment for their violations, she thought, though all four, and various others, volubly and publicly disagreed that Lettie was in the right.

Around the second week, Lettie began to notice an increase in the socializing of her neighbors. Mid-week potluck dinner parties and weekend barbecues by the pool occurred more frequently than ever. How often, when she made her rounds, did it appear that a good number of the neighbors were congregated in one unit or another? She wondered how people knew where and when to gather. Notices of these get-togethers were never posted on the information board above the mailboxes, as they had been when Lettie first moved in. Lettie checked the board every evening when she collected her mail. Mail, by the way, which never contained a formal invitation.

Lettie continued her rounds. On night eighteen, she discovered that all of the shopping carts were lined up in front of the elevator door. They were still there the following morning. On night nineteen, music seemed to blast from every unit. It wasn't until the twentieth night, when there was a trash bag outside every door, that Lettie fully understood that there was a conspiracy among her neighbors to taunt her for her efforts.

This wasn't the first time in her life that Lettie had been ostracized by a collection of slackers because the rules must be enforced. For the remainder of the school year after Ralphy Hallmeyer stole first place for his painting with a green sky, no one had sat with Lettie at lunchtime. Sure, it hurt. Indeed, at the office where it was her job to oversee code compliance, she received not one single compliment on her new wardrobe. So what if she didn't have a lot of friends? Doing what was correct and insisting that others follow the rules as well demanded a certain strength of character. Besides, what right-minded person would want to be friends with rule violators?

Before she went to bed on night twenty-one, Lettie typed the biggest batch of infraction letters yet. The longest one contained photographs. A certain neighbor, retired on a disability pension because of a back injury, apparently had recovered sufficiently to install ceramic tile in his kitchen, all by himself.

On night twenty-two, just after ten, Lettie went out as usual on her rounds. She wore a lovely work-casual pants and sweater set she had picked up on her way home, instead of the usual jeans and sweats. Her clothes felt crisp and new, part of the institutionalization of her role. The evening was fine and clear, the air was scented with early blooming jasmine. A full moon illuminated every nook on the condo grounds. That night, Lettie felt a heightened sense of expectation. What would her neighbors have thought up for her? In a strange way, she felt embraced by their antics. Their actions were acknowledgement that they knew right from wrong.

Lettie didn't have to venture far to discover the day's plot against her and code enforcement. The rules clearly said that all patio lights should be white. But every one of her neighbors, even old Mr. Edwards on his crutches, had screwed red bulbs into the outside fixtures. At first she was hurt by the scope of the mischief, and then she felt flattered; someone had gone to a great deal of trouble on her behalf.

Alone, but feeling the eyes of everyone who lived in the condo, Lettie walked through a red-lit evening, making her notes.

Resolve to continue gave way to dismay as she moved from patio gate to patio gate. For all the energy she put into enforcement, the usual carelessness still prevailed. The same non-conforming table on a patio, the same soft music emanating from unit eight, the same overweight dog. At the elevator there was an abandoned grocery cart.

Lettie was profoundly disappointed by what she saw. She was tired of making rounds and staying up late to write her letters. The net effect of her labors? Nothing, except that the neighbors seemed to have bonded.

Worst of all, the party that night was at Carlisle Jones's unit. For weeks there had been workmen and deliveries as Carlisle Jones redecorated. Lettie wanted very much to see what Jones had done inside. But most of all, Lettie wanted to be included; some vestige of her first, vain, hope that the two of them could be friends, remained. From outside the gate, Lettie could smell the food she knew would be delicious. She smoothed the front of her new sweater. Was this not the perfect outfit for a neighborhood party?

At one point Lettie actually put her hand on Carlisle Jones's patio gate, but could not screw the courage to walk inside and join the party. Everyone was inside Jones's unit, except her. Even the chubby dog was being entertained. Lettie observed various people regularly slip the little pudge morsels of high-fat delicacies. Why not just walk in? she thought. She drew back when she realized that Jones had fashioned a canopy over the entire patio out of strands of red fairy lights, and that the red lights were meant as a message to Lettie: go away.

After a deep sigh, she looked up into the night sky. Horror of all horrors, the sky glowed green! Lettie knew this was a phenomenon caused when eyes get a longish exposure to red light, and that the sky was indeed not actually green. Knowing this did not ease her enormous discomfiture one bit. Even her own eyes taunted her; under certain circumstances, skies could appear green. Skies could be green.

Sometimes epiphany comes too late.

The following morning, the offending cart was parked exactly where it had been the night before. Not only was it abandoned, but also it was not empty — against the rules — and its contents leaked a definitely non-rules-conforming fluid.

Carlisle Jones came out of her unit dressed in a sharply tailored suit. She stopped at unit four to return a chafing dish she had borrowed the day before from Mr. Oliver, the geology professor.

"Lovely meal last night," he said. "Wonderful evening. Thank you."

"My pleasure," she said. "I do enjoy having people in."

"Perhaps, if you don't have plans tomorrow, I may reciprocate." He picked up his own briefcase, put his arm through hers and walked beside her. "There's a new tandoori place I've wanted to try."

"Sounds wonderful."

Together, they stopped at Mr. Edwards's unit to drop off a covered bowl of leftovers; his leg was giving him discomfort so he missed Carlisle Jones's dinner. Leo the sax player sat in the sun on his patio, kanoodling on his horn. As they passed, he rose, stood by his gate and played them out with a riff from "Big Butter and Egg Man." The chubby dog across the way barked his greeting. The gardener, who was washing down the walkways, waved.

When Carlisle Jones and Oliver the geologist reached the elevator and saw the offending cart, and Lettie with it, they stopped short. Though Lettie's new work-casual pants and sweater set had hardly a wrinkle, Lettie herself was a mess.

"How awful," Jones said.

"Indeed." Oliver said.

"Who could be responsible?"

"The question," Oliver said, "is who among us could *not* be responsible?"

They exchanged small, conspiratorial smiles.

"Rain or shine, carts must be returned to the rubbish room." Jones pushed the elevator call button. "Don't you agree?"

"Indeed. And rubbish must be properly deposited." Oliver grasped the handle of the cart and pushed it into the elevator. The three of them rode down together: Carlisle Jones, Oliver the geologist, and Lettie the snitch. As they passed the mailboxes, both Jones and Oliver dropped letters into the out-going mail slot: Jones, a check to the DMV to cover both her fine and her new-resident car registration fees, Oliver a sharp response to demands from his wife's divorce attorney.

"May I?" Jones opened the heavy rubbish room doors. Without turning on the lights, Oliver pushed the cart inside. Together, they lifted its well-dressed contents into the big rubbish bin and then, with a hose, backtracked, washing away the deep red non-rules-conforming fluid trail the cart's contents had dribbled.

"What about the blood upstairs?" Jones asked. "Hate to leave a mess."

"The gardener will take care of it."

Jones slipped her hand through Professor Oliver's arm as they strolled together toward her car. "Where is this new tandoori place?"

ESSENTIAL THINGS

The house had good bones. That's what the Realtor said when she first brought Mike Flint to see the "handyman's dream" in the woods on the Humboldt Coast of Northern California. Good bones, meaning the foundation and frame may be salvageable, if no other parts of the house were. Termites, time, weather and neglect had all taken their toll. But if the essentials, the bones, were indeed sound, Mike thought the house had potential.

As they walked from room to room the Realtor talked about financing terms and short closing date, and Mike made notes. There were two small, dark bedrooms, one worn-out utilitarian bathroom, a good-sized combination kitchen and living room, the best feature of which was a handsome river stone fireplace. The cabin was habitable, but just barely, and only because it was summer. Before winter, if he bought the place, Mike figured he would need to put on a new roof, clean nests out of the chimney, replace the uneven linoleum floor, caulk and weather strip every opening. The list of necessary repairs was long, and there were only a few months to work before the rainy season settled in.

Mike walked through the house twice, and then he walked around outside, doing the potential home buyer's equivalent of kicking the tires. The cedar shingle siding was almost black with age and weathering, was spongy with dry rot. The siding would have to go. So would the covered porch, with its sagging roof and precarious southward tilt. If he bought the house — if — the first project would be to tear down as much of the external walls as possible and install lots of big windows, maybe French doors, to enhance the little house's singular selling feature: location. Behind the house, towering redwood forest, in front, an unobstructed view of the Pacific. If he could bring the view inside, then the house would be a gem.

"I'll take it," Mike announced.

The abruptness of his statement caught the Realtor off guard. She still had some sales pitch to deliver, and could not stop herself before a little more dribbled out. "I know it's isolated out here, but ..."

"Isolated suits me fine," he said. "I put in twenty-five years, three months and five days with the LAPD. That's a lot of years, a lot of people, and too much freeway. What I'm looking for is peace and quiet and room to move around without knocking into someone. And I want it as soon as I can get it."

"Isolated you shall have." The Realtor smiled, almost laughed; the commission was a sure thing, she could relax. She locked the front door and they headed across the hard-packed dirt front yard to the driveway where she had parked her Volvo station wagon, walking fast, both of them eager to consummate the sale.

"LAPD, you said?" She fished for her car keys. "How many people have you shot?"

"Most cops go their whole careers and never fire their weapons except on the shooting range when they qualify." He hated that tired old question, the honest answer to which would explain why he was in such a hurry to get out of Los Angeles, permanently. She was waiting for him to say something more. He took a breath. "The last eighteen years, I worked detectives, Robbery-Homicide Division. Spent most of my time wearing out shoe leather or getting a cauliflower ear from talking on the telephone all day."

She seemed skeptical, and she was persistent. "So, you never shot anyone?"

"Did I say that?"

"Actually, no, you didn't."

"Let's leave it at that, okay?"

"Whatever you say." She unlocked the car door for him. "But I bet you have stories. Policemen always have stories."

"Not me. I was just a civil servant."

"Right." She looked at him askance, evaluating him, he thought. Or judging him. "Maybe you need a beer or two to remember them, but I know you have stories."

"One or two." He smiled. "I forgot your name."

"Maureen O'Kelly."

"Nice doing business with you, Maureen O'Kelly."

As they turned from the long drive onto the cliff-top road, he took a better look at her. He decided she was an attractive woman, in an earth mother sort of way. Birkenstocks, drapey, shapeless, homespun-looking dress, long, tousled hair, earrings as big as wind chimes, no make-up, she belonged to this place the way that the hard-bodied, hard-boiled women he had worked with for twenty-five years — D.A.'s and women cops, mostly — belonged to the city. In his experience, women who dressed like Maureen O'Kelly were always marching for some radical cause or another, or promoting tofu in school lunches or some damn thing. But up here, neo-hippie seemed to be the norm. He caught himself staring at her; new possibilities for life in a new place belatedly occurred to him, and he began to relax.

"As soon as we get back into town, will you get in touch with the owner?" Mike asked, awed even as he tried to focus on practical matters, by the magnificent, wild scenery passing by outside the car. "I'd like to know the soonest I can take possession. Need to get started with repairs right away, if I'm going to live in that wreck."

"The owner of record is the U. S. of A.," she answered. "The previous owner engaged in the primary local cash commerce, growing the jolly weed, the emjay, Maria Juanita, and got caught."

He chuckled. "Quite a vocabulary for a single commodity."

"The Eskimos have a hundred words for snow, because that's what they have the most of." She smiled, and he liked the way the corners of her eyes crinkled, as if she smiled a lot. She said, "The DEA confiscated this property and now offers it to you. That's why the price is so reasonable."

"What I know about working with the federal government is red tape."

"Don't worry," she reassured him. "The feds want the quickest close possible. The gov is maintaining a vast number of properties acquired by confiscation. They're very happy and very cooperative when they get the opportunity to unload some. Your financing is in order. It's just a matter now of signing a mountain of documents and recording the sale. You can probably come by and pick up the keys at the end of next week."

"Next week?" He was surprised how high those words made his spirits soar. It was going to happen, he told himself, clenching his fists to keep from shouting out loud. It was going to happen. He'd drive back down to LA one last time, pack the essentials, dispose of the rest and be gone for good. While he dreaded perhaps making one last run through the gauntlet of vulture press that had been hanging out around the apartment he rented when he and Maggie MacGowen broke up, he took heart knowing that in a week he could be ready to take ownership of his own small piece of this primal paradise.

New lists: building materials, some plants for the front yard. What sort of plants? The soil was thin and the woods around his house were too dense and dark to grow anything except bracken ferns and mushrooms. He asked Maureen O'Kelly, "Where did the previous owner grow his crop?"

"Up in the hills somewhere," Maureen said, shrugging. "There are marijuana fields hidden all over the area. Some are really very large.

Plantations. You want to be careful if you go hiking too far into the woods, because the growers are very edgy and they pack a lot of heat."

She turned to him and smiled. "Isn't that what you police say, pack heat?"

"Only if we want to get laughed at."

"Anyway, the growers won't bother you if you don't bother them. The big commercial growers fly in and out during the night and we never see anything of them. But there are some small-time entrepreneurs, and they're usually the ones who get into trouble. With the timber industry nearly dead, there are a lot of people scraping by on public assistance. When one of them suddenly starts driving around in a big new truck or spends the winter in Hawaii, the County Sheriff and the DEA start making inquiries. That's what happened to your predecessor, he suddenly looked too prosperous for a man living on disability checks."

"He certainly wasn't spending anything on the house," Mike said.

"Not on his house, but you should see the girlfriend's house." She gave him a conspiratorial glance. "The wife turned him in."

It was noon when they got back to town. Document signing in the realty office took a little over an hour. Mike invited Maureen to join him for dinner later to celebrate the deal. There were two restaurants in town, a steak and chophouse next door to her small office, and a fish shack down by the commercial boat dock at the end of Main Street. She chose steak over fish, and they agreed to meet at the restaurant at 6:00.

To fill the rest of the day, Mike borrowed Maureen's large tape measure and drove himself back out to the house to take some measurements and poke around. He discovered that at one time the cabin had been one large room and that the bedroom walls were only flimsy drywall partitions that could be easily removed. Living in one big, high-celinged room appealed to him. By the time he met Maureen for dinner, he had plans for the renovation clear in his mind: take out the interior partitions and the dropped ceiling, surround the outside with a wide, raised deck, replace solid exterior walls with rows of French doors, install a new hardwood floor, add skylights and a sleeping loft..

By the time the rainy season began, the exterior should be finished, and the house would be tight against the cold. During the winter, he would work inside, remodeling the bathroom and kitchen, paneling the inside walls. For some projects he would need help — maybe some of the unemployed lumberjacks in town would jump at the chance to collect a few weeks of pay — but he would do as much of the work by himself as he could; it would be his house. Mike figured the total cost of the remodel, doubled it, and knew he had enough in the bank to pay for what he wanted to do and cover some unexpected contingencies without taking out an additional loan.

At dinner, it seemed as if half the town stopped by their table to greet Maureen O'Kelly and check out the stranger dining with her. The variety among the locals was a pleasant surprise to Mike: retired people, hippies frozen in time, college professors who commuted to a not-too-distant state university, commercial fishermen, some week-enders, and urban refugees like himself. The one thing they all seemed to have in common was a genuine, unguarded friendliness. Or was it nosiness? Didn't matter, because it amounted to the same thing. There would be decent enough people around.

When he first decided to get out of Dodge, i.e. Los Angeles, Mike's only thought was to find solitude, to bury himself after an epoch of brutal public scrutiny when his name came up during a nasty police scandal. With Maureen O'Kelly as his guide, he began to see himself once again as part of a community. He was afraid to let himself believe completely that a fresh start was possible, but he began to open to the notion.

They capped the evening with drinks at Maloney's, the only bar in town. Maloney's crowd was noticeably rougher than the restaurant people were. Denim and flannel, work boots, gaps among teeth, a lot of slurred speech and, in dark corners, some sloppy stolen kisses. This was the lumberjack crowd. A few times voices rose to that particular pitch and volume that made Mike reflexively put his hand on the hip where for twenty-five years he had holstered a 9mm automatic. The second time he reached for the gun that wasn't there anymore, Maureen put her hand on his arm.

"Relax. No one fights in Maloney's bar."

As if on cue, to demonstrate Maloney's peacekeeping prowess, the sound of flesh smacking flesh and a woman's cry silenced the crowd. Moving fast for a big man, Maloney vaulted the bar, grabbed the offender by one arm, gripping him high up under the armpit, yanked him out of his booth, and marched him out the door. Then he went back to the booth and leaned close to the woman snuffling into a damp cocktail napkin.

"Nelly, how many times I gotta tell you two to keep that garbage out of my place?"

"He hit me," Nelly whined.

"The way you push Fred's buttons when he's tanked, I know and you know you're asking him for it. It's the same damn thing three nights a week. Now give Fred a minute to cool off, then you go find him and get yourselves home."

Maloney straightened up and Nelly slid out of the booth, whimpering, holding her hand to one side of her face. Her macramé purse dangled from her other hand. She opened the door to leave, but before stepping out she turned and proclaimed, "He hit me."

Someone murmured, "Yeah, yeah." Someone else called out, "Goodnight, Nelly," as if nothing had happened. "Drive careful."

Mike turned from this drama to find Maureen watching him.

"You think you'll fit in around here?" she asked.

"Just like home," he chuckled. "Just like home."

The week in Los Angeles was grueling, but not as bad as it could have been, because always in the back of his mind there was the beautiful picture of the little house in the Humboldt woods. Even two days of grand jury testimony couldn't spoil his hopefulness. When he wasn't in court, Mike kept busy taking care of all the details involved with retiring and moving, too busy to let anything get him down. On Thursday, before dawn, when he pulled out of the apartment's underground garage, towing a U-Haul trailer behind his SUV, no one seemed to notice he was going. Certainly no one followed him.

As he drove, he found the trailer load was surprisingly light. Only the essentials from his past life; how few, he found, there were.

Mike stopped in Santa Rosa, the closest major city to his new home, still almost four hours drive north, and ordered building supplies to be delivered to the property. Two truckloads of lumber and windows, nails and bolts, shingles and tiles, pipes, tools, indeed even a kitchen sink. The sun had just dropped below the horizon when he arrived at Maureen O'Kelly's office to pick up his keys.

For two weeks, Mike camped out in the house. He set up his bed in the middle of the living room, hung a mosquito net from the ceiling beam above it more to keep out dust than bugs, filled the old refrigerator with provisions, and went to work. Every day, from first light until last, he labored. When it was too dark to work, he showered, ate something, and fell into bed exhausted. Every morning felt like a fresh start.

The first task was demolition. Mike stripped away dark and rotten siding until only the naked house frame remained, pulled down the flimsy interior partitions until the only privacy to be had was behind the bathroom door, removed the sagging old porch that obstructed the view of the Pacific.

There was another sort of demolition going on at the same time. As he worked, alone, Mike began to chip away at the layers of anger and guilt, resentment and grief that had driven him to seek refuge. The good bones of the house emerged from neglect in parallel with insight: a terrible thing happened a long time ago because Mike made a mistake. A well intentioned act flipped out of his control and into something ugly. No denying the outcome was bad, but the incident, as retold by a corrupt cop as part of a plea bargain, was made to seem base and vile, perhaps could be interpreted as criminal. Mike did not, would not, excuse himself for his part. But he refused to accept blame or feel guilt for more than his share. One small essential truth became clear to him as the structure of lies and emotion fell away: you cannot help people who do not want to be helped.

Physical labor and time to think made Mike feel lighter, stronger. At night he slept in the skeletal house with nothing except the mosquito net between him and the susurrus of the forest on one side, the pounding of the ocean on the other, and the deep velvet black sky above. In the morning he woke to find deer in the yard, and squirrels in the kitchen helping themselves to whatever he had neglected to put away the night before.

Every few days, he would drive into town for dinner or drinks with Maureen. Easily, he came to know a dozen or so locals by name, began to feel included in the rhythms of the place. The market closed at five, the filling station/video store at seven. By ten, an hour after the steak house stopped serving dinner, the ongoing, alcohol-fueled war between Nelly and Fred would reach the point of blows and Maloney would throw them out. Mike could measure how many days since he'd seen them by how much Nelly's bruises and Fred's scratches would fade from one sighting to the next.

At the end of the second week, Maureen dropped by to check on Mike's progress with the house. She brought zucchini and tomatoes from her garden and some halibut a neighbor had caught off the Oregon coast the day before. They cooked on the grill Mike set up in the front yard, and ate by candlelight as the last blue light of dusk faded to star-filled night. She was still there at first light. Mike rose, as had become his habit, put on his heavy gloves and went to work while she slept, sheltered inside the gossamer net.

She emerged at about nine, bringing him a cup of coffee.

"You've lost weight," she said. "You're skinny as a rail."

"I was getting awfully soft." He patted his belly and felt a sort of pride in how hard it had grown. As he sipped hot coffee, he looked up at the house. "I've done just about everything I can do by myself. Any ideas where I can hire some help?"

She smiled the way people do when they aren't sure how you're going to take what it is you have to say.

He said, "There seem to be lots of unemployed people in the area. I expect some will be happy to earn a few weeks wages."

"Indeed," she said. "But let's remember where you are. You'll find a good work crew. But help tends to disappear during the harvest season. And, my dear, this is harvest season."

"I'll take my chances," he said. "I don't have a lot of options."

Mike hand printed a workers-wanted flyer, made copies in Maureen's office and posted them in Maloney's bar and various other visible places in town. The following morning six men showed up at his house, the following day four more. On the third day, no one. This became the pattern. Men showed up en masse, or no one came, and it did Mike no good to try to bribe them or cajole them or even serve good lunches. When they came, the townsmen worked hard and showed great skill. When they didn't? Mike had the day to himself.

Mike worked out a system. He could not compete with the wages paid by marijuana growers who needed to get a crop harvested. But on those days when the growers had enough men or the weather made picking impossible, or perhaps federal agents showed up, then Mike would have a crew. For this possibility he always had building materials ready and a sequence of jobs prioritized so that progress was made.

There was a sort of serial barn raising in effect. Large numbers of men put in all the French doors and exterior walls over three days, built the new deck in two, installed the roof over two more. Each of these heady occasions was a full week or ten days apart, but accomplished the same amount of work that a small crew, working daily, would have managed in a similar expanse of time. The greatest benefit to Mike was that he bonded with a good number of his neighbors; sometimes, his need to be alone scared him.

On those occasions when no one showed up, Mike did finish work, or made the trip down to Santa Rosa for building supplies, or filled his SUV with rubbish and drove out to the county landfill. Now and then he took a day off, signed on with a deep-sea charter and went fishing just to feel the power of the ocean under him. He decided to start looking for a boat to buy. Maybe the feds also confiscated little fishing boats, he thought, and made a mental note to ask Maureen.

It was on a trip to the county landfill one morning that Mike met the county sheriff. The back of Mike's SUV was jammed with green plastic trash bags, so jammed he couldn't see through his rearview mirror. Indeed, didn't know the sheriff was following him until he heard the bleat of a siren.

Mike handed over his car registration and his driver's license, which was conveniently tucked next to his retired peace officer card.

The sheriff, a man about Mike's age, wore a green shirt, blue jeans and hiking boots. His hair was much too long to pass muster at the LAPD, but his body was lean and hard, as a patrolman's body should be. Briefly, he studied Mike's documents, studied Mike, then he studied the heap of bags in Mike's truck.

"Quite a load," the sheriff said.

"Construction rubbish."

"Yeah?" The sheriff reached past Mike's shoulder to prod a bag. "Around here I see a truck full of trash bags I assume it's something else."

"Sorry to disappoint."

"You bought the Peterson place." This was a statement, not a question. In answer to the obvious question, he said, "Maureen O'Kelly is my wife's cousin. Besides that, there are no secrets in a small town."

The sheriff handed back Mike's license, then he offered his hand. "Paul Savoie," he said. "Nice to meet you. Welcome to town."

"Thanks."

"I know who are. I've been following what's going on down there in La La land." Sheriff Savoie leaned against the side the SUV, settling in for a nice, long talk. "You've had it pretty rough."

"Guess it was my turn." Mike got out and leaned against the SUV as well, because it was clear he wouldn't be leaving any time soon, and the car was hot inside.

"Yep." Savoie pulled a pouch of Bull Durham and a packet of ZigZags out of his shirt pocket and deftly rolled a cigarette. "Pretty rough."

Savoie blew a thin stream of smoke out one side of his mouth. "I worked patrol in Oakland for a dozen years before I applied up here. More than a few things happened back then that I would just as soon never got out. Official procedure and basic street cop survival aren't always compatible."

"Not always," Mike said.

"What's happening to you could happen to any of us. Too bad this time it's you."

For three-quarters of an hour they swapped stories about the old days when, they agreed, kicking butt and taking names kept the streets safer than the kinder, gentler mode of modern police work. Above all, Mike felt relieved to have someone to talk to who understood how sometimes situations can get out of control; the human behavior variable is infinite. Leaning against the side of his SUV, morning sun slanting through a leafy redwood canopy overhead, Mike opened up, and for the first time told his version of what happened without constraint or embarrassment or fear of incriminating himself.

"The kid was seventeen, but he was no kid," Mike said. "Six-six, two-eighty. His mother was a little bitty thing, five feet max. Before he was ten, he could throw her over his shoulder. She did her best, all things considered, but she lost him to the street, like she lost her older boy, too. The kid tried crank and meth and I don't know what all, but it was alcohol he had taste for. And alcohol made him mean."

Mike continued. "When the kid couldn't steal enough to stay drunk, he'd terrorize his mother until she gave him the grocery money. On the day her check came, he'd be there waiting. If she balked, he beat her. If she gave in, he'd get drunk, come home and beat her. I don't know how many times we rolled on calls to her house to rescue her from her own kid. I told you he was big; when he was high it took three of us to take him down. She'd call us for help, but when we tried to help her by getting the kid out, she'd turn on us. We'd be wrestling this chunk of boy, and she'd be right in there, pounding on us, 'Don't hurt my baby. Don't hurt my baby.'

"We'd book him, she'd bail him out before he sobered up, take him home, they'd start in all over again. I can't count the number of times we rolled on calls to her house two, three times in a single night. Let him spend the weekend in the slam, we'd say, give yourself a break. Give him time to sleep it off. Nothing we said to her made a difference. She kept bailing him out."

"She loved him." Savoie crushed a butt under his toe and rolled another. "I know how that goes. I hate domestic calls. People ask for your help, then they get in the way when you try."

"Yeah." Mike closed his eyes, seeing the woman's tiny fists pounding him as he tried to cuff the kid. He said, "Frankly, I got tired of it. We told her that if something didn't change, one of those nights we'd be calling the coroner to come get her."

"What did you do?"

"The kid had a big brother who was taken out by a rival gang and dumped in a vacant field four, five miles down the freeway. My partner and I picked up Junior, drunk, first of the month, right on schedule. He'd had enough to drink that he passed out in the back seat. That night, instead of taking him in and booking him, we drove him to this field where his brother's body had been found and we dumped him there. The idea was that when he woke up and realized where he was, he might think things over. If nothing else, he'd have time to sober up and Mom would have a night off. We'd get a night off."

"Didn't work out that way?"

"He never got home."

Savoie nodded. "Bullet in the head, is that what I read?"

"Yes."

"Who did it?"

"Not me, that's all I know." Mike looked off into the woods, remembering.

"Never found the shooter?" Savoie asked.

"No one looked very hard. Not then." Mike turned to Savoie. "What it all comes down to is this: The way the kid lived, where the kid lived, you knew he wasn't going to die an old man. Don't get me wrong, every day of my life I regret what happened to him and any part I played in his passing. I don't know if his mother would agree, but I can't help but believe his untimely departure spared a lot of people a lot of grief. Me included."

"You're probably right." Savoie nodded knowingly. "You're probably right."

Savoie got into the habit of dropping by Mike's house a couple of days a week for a beer and talk after his patrol shift. He turned out to be a decent finish carpenter and helped Mike miter and install crown molding. More importantly, he helped Mike work through doubts about the condition of his immortal soul: things happen on patrol that only another cop would understand.

Right away, they became two couples, Mike and Maureen, Savoie and his wife Janis. Barbecues, berrying, fishing, every few weeks a drive up the coast to the picturesque town of Ferndale for a movie. By Fall Mike felt like a local.

The light changed, days grew shorter, evenings chillier. When the first rainstorm came, Mike was ready. The house was warm and tight against the rain that blew in off the Pacific. Wind whipped the redwoods around his house into dancing frenzies, but not even a little draft could be felt inside. Mike worked contentedly indoors. He sealed and polished the new hardwood floor, loved how it reflected the glow from the fireplace. Paneled the walls.

The sleeping loft also gave him great satisfaction. He built it across the opposite end of the room from the fireplace, a gallery under the slope of the roof, accessed by ladder. With a skylight above his bed and windows all around, on clear nights he could lie on his back and see the glint of moonlight on the ocean, the feathery blackness of tree tops, and a sky filled with more stars than he, as a city boy, imagined existed. During the storm, he fell asleep to the sound of rain, wakened to the sound of water dripping from the trees, a secondary rainfall that lasted all day.

At around seven on the morning the sun came out again, Mike looked up from his breakfast to see Paul Savoie's sheriff patrol car turn into his driveway. Curious, he put on his slicker and walked out to meet him.

"I need a big city detective to take a look at something." Savoie pulled up beside Mike, spoke through his open car window. "Hop in. I'd like to hear what you have to say."

"What happened?" Mike asked.

"That's what I want you to help me figure out."

Mike climbed in and Savoie drove them to the far side of town and up a narrow unpaved road that wound into the hills. The scattering of houses in the woods grew sparser the further they drove. They came around a curve, and just where the road began to incline steeply, two pickup trucks blocked the road: an old blue Chevy headed downhill, and, maybe ten yards in front of it, there was a brand new, bright red pickup truck headed uphill, the driver side door hanging open.

Mike recognized the new red truck as the one the town squabblers, Fred and Nelly, had started driving late in the summer. There had been quite a bit of discussion in town about how Fred could afford such a vehicle on his disability pension, and the usual speculation about what he might be doing on the side for money. The conversation about what he might be up to and whom he might be involved with had suddenly become quite pertinent: Fred was pinned under the front tires of his truck. From the angle of his neck and the definite concave shape his once burly chest had acquired, it was obvious even at a distance that the next call would be to the mortuary in Ferndale, not to the hospital.

A local named Arnold Aufwald, who belonged to the other truck, an older Chevy, sat on a rock beside the road, puffing on a pipe. Savoie pulled up twenty feet behind the red truck. When he and Mike got out of the patrol car, Arnold rose from his perch and sauntered over to meet them.

Out of habit, Mike began studying the scene even before they got out of the car. There was a single set of tire tracks behind the red truck, and a confusion of footprints around the open driver side door. Mike looked down at the impression Arnold's Red Star work boots made in the mud, looked at his own tracks and at Savoie's as a way of separating prints made during the discovery of the body from those perhaps left during the event that put it there.

"No one came by at all, Sheriff," Arnold said. "Saturday mornings, folks in this neck of the woods are still sleeping off Friday nights."

Mike saw a folded twenty palmed in the hand Savoie extended to Arnold. "Appreciate you standing watch. Wouldn't want anyone wandering through before I could get here."

"Any time." Arnold slipped the twenty into his jeans pocket and repeated, "Any time."

"You know Mike Flint," Savoie said.

"Seen him in town," Arnold said, offering Mike his hand. "Hear you're spending time with Maureen O'Kelly. Nice lady. Sold us our house a couple years back. You've put in a lot of work on the old Peterson place."

"Tell us what you know, Arnold," Savoie said, interrupting.

Arnold gestured toward the red truck with his pipe. "I was driving down to the dock this morning to work on my boat, when I ran into Fred." He blushed furiously and rushed to correct himself. "Don't mean I actually ran into Fred, just that I couldn't get past his truck in the road here. I pulled up, saw Fred down under there. I thought at first he was having some tire trouble or a broken axle, so I went over to see if he needed help." Then he shrugged as if the rest was self-evident. "I called it in on the CB in my truck, talked to the Sheriff, and here you are."

"Hear anything last night?"

"Just the storm."

"Thanks," Savoie said. "Stick around a little longer, if you don't mind, in case we have some questions."

Arnold shrugged, went back to sit on his rock, relit his pipe and watched the other two with open curiosity. There would be plenty to talk about in town for weeks; Arnold had discovered a body.

Savoie took out a Polaroid camera and began to take pictures of the scene. Being careful care not to disturb the tire tracks or existing footprints, Mike made his way toward the truck where Fred lay, face up, arms flung to the side as if he were making mud angels under there. Mike got down on one knee, picked up Fred's hand, found it stiff, touched the side of his neck, found it cold. Touched the hood of the truck, cold as well. Then he looked inside the cab. The gearshift was in park, keys were in the ignition, and there was a half-empty bottle of Four Roses on the front seat.

He caught Sheriff Savoie watching him with a wry grin on his face. "And?"

"There are footprints leading from the driver's door to the front of the truck, but Arnold obliterated any from the bumper forward," Mike said. "You might be able to make castings and sort them out."

"Might."

"What time did it stop raining last night?" Mike asked.

"Around midnight," Savoie said.

"Then whatever happened, happened after midnight. Otherwise the tracks would have washed away."

"Seems so."

"Fred's in full rigor. It was cool last night, so onset would be slow. A liver thermometer and a weather report would help, but I'm guessing he's been dead at least six hours.

"That narrows things. Maloney threw Fred and Nelly out at ten — fighting as usual — it's seven-thirty now," Savoie said. "But time of death, cause of death, they aren't the real issues here, are they?"

Mike shook his head.

"Accidental or intentional?"

"Hard to say," Mike said. "Trucks can't roll uphill."

"Down there in the big city, how would you proceed?"

"Where's Nelly?"

The mortician in Ferndale held the office of county coroner, a matter of convenience. The mortuary hearse picked up Fred's remains shortly after ten, just about the same time a crime scene investigator from sheriff headquarters arrived. Excused from the scene after debriefing, Mike and Savoie drove a quarter mile up the road to Fred and Nelly's cabin.

The cabin was deep in the woods, an eyesore well hidden from the road. When Mike saw that the front door was wide open, he felt the old familiar surge from his years on the job. Something bad happened; what would they find inside?

Savoie banged on the doorjamb and called out, "Nelly! Nelly, you here?"

Mike went in after their second and third knocks brought no response. He found Nelly in a dead sprawl on the bed she doubtless shared with Fred. One shoe on, mud to her knees, hair a tangled mess. Mike was feeling for a pulse in her neck when she stirred.

"Wha'?" Nelly lifted her head and looked at Mike, confused, reeking of alcohol, fresh shiner on her right eye, she was quite a picture. She started to say, "Where?" but seemed to realize where she was, so she said, "Who?"

Paul Savoie came up beside Mike.

"Sheriff?" she said, still confused.

"What happened last night, Nelly?" he asked.

She raised her hand to shield her eyes from the light at the window behind Mike, touched the shiner and flinched. "Damn Fred. He hit me."

"I spoke with Maloney this morning," Savoie said. "He said you and Fred really got into it last night."

She shrugged. "You know how Fred gets when he's had a few drinks."

"What did you do after you left Maloney's?"

The effort to remember seemed to hurt. At last she said, "Came home."

"Straight home?"

"More or less. Fred had a bottle in the truck. We drove down to the dock and had a little nightcap. Then we came home. Why?"

"How did you get home, Nelly?"

"Drove."

"In the truck?"

"Yes, in the truck." She seemed puzzled. "Don't have another vehicle. How else would we get home?"

Savoie pointed at her mud-encrusted feet and jeans. "You could have walked."

She studied her shoeless foot for clues. "All the way from town?"

"From the road."

The suggestion seemed to jog something loose from her besotted memory bank. She looked at the bed beside her, the gray shadow on the sheet that likely defined Fred's usual place beside her.

" Oh yeah," she said, at last, nodding. "I think I did walk from the road."

"Why did you walk? Was there a problem with the truck?"

"No." She made an exaggerated frown, unclear, it appeared, about the sequence of events. "The problem was with Fred. He was going on about something. I don't remember what, but I guess I didn't want to hear it anymore. I told him to stop the truck and let me out ."

"Did he stop the truck?"

"He stopped the truck and took a shot at me." She touched her shiner gingerly and turned her head to show it to Savoie. "How bad is it?"

"I've seen worse," Savoie said.

Mike asked, "When he hit you, were you in the truck or outside?"

"Out," she said after some thought. "I got out. We had a bottle, and I snagged it. That's when he hit me. Because I took the bottle."

"Then what happened?" Savoie asked.

"Nothing." She looked from Savoie to Mike. "I guess I walked home. Next thing I know, you're waking me up. Who are you, anyway? Do I know you?"

Nelly started to sit up, stopped halfway to rub her forehead, then managed to get upright. "Damn, I need coffee. Fred!" she shouted in the general direction of the open bedroom doorway. "Freddie, baby, put some coffee on, will you?"

Mike watched Nelly's reaction when Savoie told her Fred had been in an accident. Confusion, concern, finally grief, but nothing that looked like consciousness of guilt. Over the course of the day, as her head cleared, she might remember more about what happened the night before. Or she might not. Mike didn't think it really mattered.

They waited outside while Nelly pulled herself together enough to make the trip to Ferndale.

"In the big city," Savoie said, "what would you do with this situation?"

"Write a report." Mike shrugged. "Send it into the system with no recommendation, knowing it would get lost. We'll never know exactly how Fred got under those wheels, but I don't see evidence of criminal act or intent. What are you going to do?"

"Write a report, file it," Savoie said. "Go home, make potato salad for Fred's wake. Go to the funeral."

"Probably best that way."

"It's like what you said about that kid, the way he lived you knew he wasn't going to die an old man."

The day after Fred's funeral was bright and warm, like a second coming of summer. Sheriff Savoie and his wife Janis, Mike and Maureen borrowed a pair of two-person kayaks and rowed out toward the open sea, setting out from the commercial fishing dock at the end of Main Street. Getting past the line of breakers was hard work, but once they were clear, the ocean rolled gently under them. The water was frigid, but the sun was so bright that, about half an hour into the trip, Mike stopped to take off his windbreaker. Maureen positioned the kayak to face the shore.

"Look, Mike." High up on the bluff in front of them, Mike's house shone, fresh and clean, almost shiny against the deep green of the woods behind. "I told you that house had good bones."

He leaned forward and kissed her shoulder. He knew there was still work to be done inside, and that it would take time. But the structure was now whole and strong, stronger than it had ever been. And that was the essential thing.

FICTION BY WENDY HORNSBY

NOVELS AND SHORT-STORY COLLECTION

No Harm. Dodd, Mead, 1987; Worldwide Library, 1988
Half a Mind. New American Library, 1990; Onyx, 1991
Telling Lies. Dutton, 1992; Onyx, 1993
Midnight Baby. Signet, August 1994; Dutton, June, 1993
Bad Intent. Dutton, August, 1994; Signet, 1995
77th Street Requiem. Dutton, October, 1995; Signet, August 1996
A Hard Light. Dutton, August 1997; Signet, July 1998
Nine Sons: Collected Mysteries. Crippen & Landru, February 2002.

SHORT STORIES

"Nine Sons." *Sisters in Crime 4*, Berkley, 1991 (Winner of 1992 Edgar
    Allan Poe Award, Mystery Writers of America, for Best Short
    Story)
"Wendy Goes to the Morgue" (article). *Mystery Scene*, 1992
"High Heels in the Headliner." *Malice Domestic 2*, Pocket Books, 1994
"New Moon and Rattlesnakes." *Tony Hillerman Presents, The
    Mysterious West*, HarperCollins, 1994
"Ghost Caper." *Phantoms*, Onyx, 1994
"Be Your Own Best Friend," by Wendy Hornsby and Alyson
    Hornsby. *Great Writers and Kids Write Mystery Stories*, Random
    House, 1996
"Out of Time, " by Wendy Hornsby and Alyson Hornsby. *Mothers
    and Daughters*, Signet, 1997

CHECKLIST OF WENDY HORNSBY'S FICTION

"The Naked Giant." *The Best of the Best*, Signet 1997, 50th anniversary collection

"The Last is Adoration." *Ellery Queen's Mystery Magazine*, April 2000

"The Sky Shall Always Be Blue." *Nine Sons: Collected Mysteries*, Crippen & Landru, 2002

"Essential Things." *Nine Sons: Collected Mysteries*, Crippen & Landru, 2002

"Why Vanessa Jumped." Supplement to the limited edition of *Nine Sons: Collected Mysteries*, Crippen & Landru, 2002

NINE SONS

Nine Sons: Collected Mysteries by Wendy Hornsby is printed on 60-pound Glatfelter Supple Opaque recycled acid-free paper, from 12- and 13-point Garamond. The cover painting is by Barbara Mitchell and design by Deborah Miller. The first edition comprises two hundred twenty-five copies sewn in cloth, signed and numbered by the author, and approximately eight hundred copies in trade softcover, notchbound. Each copy of the cloth edition includes a separate pamphlet, *Why Vanessa Jumped*, by Wendy Hornsby.

Nine Sons was printed and bound by Thomson-Shore, Inc., Dexter, Michigan, and published in January 2002 by Crippen & Landru Publishers, Norfolk, Virginia.

CRIPPEN & LANDRU, PUBLISHERS

P. O. Box 9315
Norfolk, VA 23505
E-mail: CrippenL@Pilot.Infi.Net
Web: www.crippenlandru.com

Crippen & Landru publishes first edition short-story collections by important detective and mystery writers. As of January 2002, the following books have been published (see our website for full details):

Speak of the Devil by John Dickson Carr. 1994. Out of print.

The McCone Files by Marcia Muller. 1995. Signed, numbered clothbound, out of print. Trade softcover, sixth printing, $17.00.

The Darings of the Red Rose by Margery Allingham. 1995. Out of print.

Diagnosis: Impossible, The Problems of Dr. Sam Hawthorne by Edward D. Hoch. 1996. Signed, numbered clothbound, out of print. Trade softcover, second printing, $15.00.

Spadework: A Collection of "Nameless Detective" Stories by Bill Pronzini. 1996. Signed, numbered clothbound, out of print. Trade softcover, temporarily out of stock.

Who Killed Father Christmas? And Other Unseasonable Demises by Patricia Moyes. 1996. Signed, numbered clothbound, out of print. A few signed unnumbered cloth overrun copies, $30.00. Trade softcover, $16.00.

My Mother, The Detective: The Complete "Mom" Short Stories, by James Yaffe. 1997. Signed, numbered clothbound, out of print. Trade softcover, $15.00.

In Kensington Gardens Once . . . by H.R.F. Keating. 1997. Signed, numbered clothbound, out of print. Trade softcover, $12.00.

Shoveling Smoke: Selected Mystery Stories by Margaret Maron. 1997. Signed, numbered clothbound, out of print. Trade softcover, third printing, $16.00.

The Man Who Hated Banks and Other Mysteries by Michael Gilbert. 1997. Signed, numbered clothbound, out of print. Trade softcover, second printing, $16.00.

The Ripper of Storyville and Other Ben Snow Tales by Edward D. Hoch. 1997. Signed, numbered clothbound, out of print. Trade softcover, out of stock.

Do Not Exceed the Stated Dose by Peter Lovesey. 1998. Signed, numbered clothbound, out of print. Trade softcover, $16.00.

Renowned Be Thy Grave; Or, The Murderous Miss Mooney by P.M. Carlson. 1998. Signed, numbered clothbound, out of print. Trade softcover, $16.00.

Carpenter and Quincannon, Professional Detective Services by Bill Pronzini. 1998. Signed, numbered clothbound, out of print. Trade softcover, second printing, $16.00.

Not Safe After Dark and Other Stories by Peter Robinson. 1998. Signed, numbered clothbound, out of print. Trade softcover, second printing, $16.00.

The Concise Cuddy, A Collection of John Francis Cuddy Stories by Jeremiah Healy. 1998. Signed, numbered clothbound, out of print. Trade softcover, out of stock.

One Night Stands by Lawrence Block. 1999. Out of print.

All Creatures Dark and Dangerous by Doug Allyn. 1999. Signed, numbered clothbound, out of print. Trade softcover, $16.00.

Famous Blue Raincoat: Mystery Stories by Ed Gorman. 1999. Signed, numbered clothbound, out of print. A few signed unnumbered cloth overrun copies, $30.00. Trade softcover, $17.00.

The Tragedy of Errors and Others by Ellery Queen. 1999. Numbered clothbound, out of print. Trade softcover, second printing, $16.00.

McCone and Friends by Marcia Muller. 2000. Signed, numbered clothbound, out of print. Trade softcover, third printing, $16.00.

Challenge the Widow Maker and Other Stories of People in Peril by Clark Howard. 2000. Signed, numbered clothbound, out of print. Trade softcover, $16.00.

The Velvet Touch: Nick Velvet Stories by Edward D. Hoch. 2000. Signed, numbered clothbound, out of print. Trade softcover, $16.00.

Fortune's World by Michael Collins. 2000. Signed, numbered clothbound, out of print. Trade softcover, $16.00.

Long Live the Dead: Tales from Black Mask by Hugh B. Cave. 2000. Signed, numbered clothbound, out of print. Trade softcover, second printing, $16.00.

Tales Out of School: Mystery Stories by Carolyn Wheat. 2000. Signed, numbered clothbound, out of print. Trade softcover, $16.00.

Stakeout on Page Street and Other DKA Files by Joe Gores. 2000. Signed, numbered clothbound, out of print. Trade softcover, second printing, $16.00.

Strangers in Town: Three Newly Discovered Mysteries by Ross Macdonald, edited by Tom Nolan. 2001. Numbered clothbound, out of print. Trade softcover, second printing, $15.00.

The Celestial Buffet and Other Morsels of Murder by Susan Dunlap. 2001. Signed, numbered clothbound, out of print. Trade softcover, $16.00.

Kisses of Death: A Nathan Heller Casebook by Max Allan Collins. 2001. Trade softcover, second printing, $17.00.

The Old Spies Club and Other Intrigues of Rand by Edward D. Hoch. 2001. Signed, numbered clothbound, $42.00. Trade softcover, $17.00.

Adam and Eve on a Raft: Mystery Stories by Ron Goulart. 2001. Signed, numbered clothbound, $42.00. Trade softcover, $17.00.

The Sedgemoor Strangler and Other Stories of Crime by Peter Lovesey. 2001. Signed, numbered clothbound, $42.00. Trade softcover, $17.00.

The Reluctant Detective and Other Stories by Michael Z. Lewin. 2001. Signed, numbered clothbound, $42.00. Trade softcover, $17.00.

The Lost Cases of Ed London by Lawrence Block. 2001. Published only in Signed, numbered clothbound, $42.00.

Nine Sons: Collected Mysteries by Wendy Hornsby. 2002. Signed, numbered clothbound, $42.00. Trade softcover, $16.00.

Forthcoming Short-Story Collections

The Newtonian Egg and Other Cases of Rolf le Roux by Peter Godfrey [A "Crippen & Landru Lost Classic"].

Jo Gar's Casebook by Raoul Whitfield [published with Black Mask Press].

The Curious Conspiracy and Other Crimes by Michael Gilbert.

Come Into My Parlor: Stories from Detective Fiction Weekly by Hugh B. Cave.

Murder, Mystery and Malone by Craig Rice, edited by Jeffrey Marks [A "Crippen & Landru Lost Classic"].

The 13 Culprits by Georges Simenon, translated by Peter Schulman.

The Dark Snow and Other Stories by Brendan DuBois.

The Iron Angel and Other Tales of Michael Vlado by Edward D. Hoch.

The Sleuth of Baghdad by Charles B. Child [A "Crippen & Landru Lost Classic"].

One of a Kind: Collected Mystery Stories by Eric Wright.

Problems Solved by Bill Pronzini and Barry N. Malzberg.

Hildegarde Withers: Uncollected Riddles by Stuart Palmer [A "Crippen & Landru Lost Classic"].

Cuddy Plus One by Jeremiah Healy.

Kill the Umpire: The Calls of Ed Gorgon by Jon L. Breen.

Banner Crimes by Joseph Commings [A "Crippen & Landru Lost Classic"]

14 Slayers by Paul Cain [published with Black Mask Press].

The Adventure of the Murdered Moths and Other Radio Mysteries by Ellery Queen.

The Mankiller of Poojeegai and Other Mysteries by Walter Satterthwait.

You'll Die Laughing by Norbert Davis, edited by Bill Pronzini [published with Black Mask Press].

The Spotted Cat and Other Mysteries from the Casebook of Inspector Cockrill by Christianna Brand [A "Crippen & Landru Lost Classic"].

Hoch's Ladies by Edward D. Hoch.

A Pocketful of Noses: Stories of One Ganelon or Another by James Powell.

Untitled collection of Slot-Machine Kelly stories by Michael Collins.

Untitled collection of historical detection by Amy Myers.

Crippen & Landru offers discounts to individuals and institutions who place Standing Order Subscriptions for its forthcoming publications, either the Regular Series or the Lost Classics or (preferably) both. Collectors can thereby guarantee receiving limited editions, and readers won't miss any favorite stories. Standing Order Subscribers receive a specially commissioned story in a deluxe edition as a gift at the end of the year. Please write or e-mail for more details.